# The Legend of Bucket Smith

# by Dan Price

*August/1965*

*The envelope was addressed to Theodore "Bucket" Smith.*

*The letter inside was smudged, wrinkled and covered in blood. The soldier had read the letter many times, but this time he thought it would be his last.*

*The soldier held on to his right elbow, his arm shook, but he managed to safely tuck the letter into a pocket in his jacket. He closed his eyes.*

*The medics rushed to his side. His bullet-riddled body was rushed from the edge of a muddy river bank into the helicopter. He heard the sound of the blades, rotating above him, as the pilot pulled back on the lever. The helicopter disappeared into the night sky. Bucket remembers the letter and little else.*

*And it was just as well.*

# Chapter 1

March/1966

"Bucket, your taxi is out front," the woman said, as she stuck her head through the hotel room doorway. "Don't forget to drop off those keys and pay me fifty bucks."

Bucket had spent three days in the rat-infested hotel and that was the most words the woman, known as Phyllis, had strung together in his behalf.

He had the fifty bucks. No problem. In fact, he still had enough money to get him home. How he would handle things once he got there was another matter.

Bits and pieces of information about his past would fade in and out of his mind. The doctors and nurses had done their part, releasing what they had on Theodore "Bucket" Smith. Still, even then, it left him with more questions than answers.

What he did know was his age. He was 25 years old. He had seen his share of duty in Vietnam. He had been in a coma. He had come back from the dead and he had most of his memory back, even though his thoughts included some nightmarish flashbacks. But he had the letter and he was heading home.

Bucket was three thousand miles from home. His ticket

showed a transfer in Memphis and again in Albuquerque, but once he settled in his seat, he figured he'd have some quiet time...some time to gather his thoughts and prepare himself for what was ahead of him. It would be a lot quieter than the taxi ride he had just taken.

"Call me, Clyde," the New York cab driver had said to him.

And that was just the beginning of the one-sided, ongoing conversation. A good hour had passed before the cab driver had finally pulled into the train station. Clyde had quickly held out his hand and waited anxiously for his money.

Bucket recalled the taxi driver's parting words. "Nice talking to you...what did you say your name is?"

The soldier cracked a smile. He had finally joined the conversation. "Bucket...Bucket Smith...thanks for the ride. Say hello to the family."

Bucket then hustled through the lobby and headed for the boarding area. He had just five minutes to spare. The taxi ride should have taken a shade over thirty minutes. Bucket figured old Clyde had pocketed an extra twenty bucks.

Once aboard, Bucket threw down his duffel bag and quickly found his aisle seat. He still had Clyde on his mind. Bucket shook his head. He knew more about Clyde and his family than he knew about his own.

Clyde's last name was Barrow. He was born and raised in New Jersey. He had six kids, four still living at home. He had a wife, who is the best cook in the world and he is a Yankee fan.

The train started to pull out of the station. The seat next to him was empty. No Clyde. Bucket dosed off. He had already succumbed to the dull, repetitious sound beneath him.

**June/1941**

For Maggie Smith the day began like any other. The sun rose up over the mountains and lit up the small town of Cordes Junction. The sky was a dark blue. The clouds, a fluffy white with a mixture of gray, moving slowly from north to south, making its way toward Black Canyon City and then on into the northern edge of Phoenix.

When the sun disappeared behind a cloud the temperature would drop quickly, but as the clouds drifted away from town, the sun would return, allowing the warmer, more comfortable air to return.

Maggie shaded her eyes. She removed a strand of her blond hair from her face. She figured there was just enough of a breeze for the clothes to dry. She kicked the laundry basket forward, took the two wooded pins out of her mouth and attached her summer dress to the wired clothes line.

She suddenly heard a noise coming from the front of the house. She heard a thump, a rattling on her wooded porch, a car door slamming shut, followed by a screeching of rubber and the roar of an engine as the automobile sped away.

Maggie dropped the laundry basket and rushed to the front of the house. She caught only the plate number on the back of the vehicle and nothing else. Why she did that, God only knows, she thought, as she sealed the number

AZ64943 in the far corner of her mind.

What she saw next would change her life forever.

She looked down and on the porch sat a huge metal bucket. The bucket moved.

Maggie covered her hands over her face and moved closer. A tiny baby squirmed inside.

She picked up the baby and held the infant in her arms. The baby was wrapped in a blanket. A single bottle, half full of milk was the only item left in the bucket.

No note. Nothing.

She glanced at the child. It was a boy! She checked his head, his arms, his feet. He was a beautiful boy.

"Why?" She muttered to herself. She yelled out. "Who could do such a thing?" She looked up the dirt road. She saw nothing but dust. Maggie held the baby tight, pushed open the screen door and rushed into the house. She picked up the phone and started to dial for help. She stopped and slowly put the phone down. Her mind was racing.

"No...no," she yelled out.

All she ever wanted was a family. A loving husband, a child, a happy home and a family to love, but those dreams were shattered years ago when Herman walked out the front door and never returned.

Herman, a hard luck gambler and a sucker for an inside straight draw or better yet a "river card" which would change four suited cards into a hand-winning flush, was drawn to the poker tables and to those hidden rooms in the back of a tavern where money was to be made if...and, it was always a big if with Herman, the cards would fall his way.

Maggie had watched Herman drive away, down the same dirt road...the same dusty road she was now looking at.

After years and years of loneliness, suddenly a beautiful baby boy is left at her doorstep. Maggie decided, right then and there... she would never be alone again.

Bucket squirmed in his seat and opened his eyes. A gray-haired black man was standing over him. The man held out his hand and in a deep voice said, "Ticket please."

"Sure thing," Bucket said, as he reached inside his coat pocket and handed the man the ticket stub.

"I see you have a transfer in Memphis. Don't miss it."

"Don't worry, Sir. I'm heading home. It's been six years. I don't plan to miss the train."

"Looks like you have about eight hours in Memphis. Don't see how you can miss it. I'll give you a nudge in a few hours when the dinner car opens up. Until then, get some shut-eye."

Bucket thanked the man and went back to sleep. Within minutes, Bucket was back in the jungle. It was that God awful dream again. Instead of hearing the screeching sound of the railroad track below he heard the blast of gunfire as bullets sizzled past his body.

Joey Henderson dove into the foxhole and crawled quickly to the soldier in charge. "Sergeant Smith we can't hold them off any more!"

"Yes, we can and we will," Bucket yelled back. "The air support is on its way. Stay close to me, Joey." "Where are the others?"

"About 200 yards to the right of us. There's no more than a dozen of us left. The rest are all gone, Sergeant Smith!"

Bucket checked his watch. "One minute to go and then our boys are going to blast that ridge. Keep your head down."

Suddenly, the night sky lit up and the shadowy ridge to the

north turned into an inferno. Then they came, one after another. Bucket and Joey unleashed every bit of ammo they had left. What seemed like an hour was one minute and forty-five seconds. Bucket looked down at his shattered watch. Less than two minutes of hell and it was over.

Bucket felt the pain first in his right leg, then in his left shoulder and finally, the worst of all, the ringing just above his right ear. "Joey, hand me the radio."

"Joey!"

Henderson was gone.

His lifeless body curled up in the far corner of the foxhole. "Medic!" Bucket cried out.

One hour passed...maybe two. Sergeant Theodore "Bucket" Smith slowly closed his eyes as dust blanketed the sky above and the helicopter hovered overhead.

## Chapter 2

## Maggie's Way

Maggie would need help. She had only one person she could trust. Mildred Dunworthy lived a mile down the road. She was in her late 60s, but a very smart woman who had spent a lifetime surviving on her own. She was artistic, very good with her hands, and she had a knack for turning small amounts of clay into beautiful pots. She also had a green thumb and her gardening skills were the talk of the county.

Mildred made a few bucks selling her goods. Every Sunday she would drive to nearby Prescott to sell her pottery and produce. It was a hard life. She was a survivor. She had to go against the establishment more than once. She might have even broken the law one time or another. She was a tough woman and the only person that Maggie could count on.

Maggie had no idea how she was going to bring up this beautiful child. Money was tight and she could barely take care of herself. She grabbed the keys to the Dodge. She overturned the basket of flowers on the coffee table and wrapped the baby in a blanket. She gently placed the child in the basket and rushed out the front door.

Mildred was working on her garden. She was very pleased on how her vegetables were doing.

The unexpected, desert showers the past few weeks had certainly helped to spruce up her handiwork. The Phoenix Gazette had been out to the house recently and had taken pictures of her monster tomatoes and had run photos in last Sunday's addition.

The woman reached for her back. The sharp pulsating pain that ran down the middle of her spine and down her right leg meant it was time to quit. That was enough hoeing for one day and besides some one had just pulled up in front of the house. She tightened her straw hat, put down the hoe and headed for the front of the house to see what all the commotion was about.

"Mildred, I need help," yelled Maggie as she rushed to the side of the old woman.

"What is it child? What's wrong?"

"It's a baby, Mildred, it's a baby!"

So it began.

Two women and a baby. Maggie and Mildred put their own wants and their own needs aside. The child who came out of nowhere became their first priority. They pooled their money. They concocted a story that would fly for a few months...maybe a few years — a story that would keep the grocery store clerk, the gossipy hairdresser and even the local sheriff from asking too many questions.

Maggie kept her job in Camp Verde. Five days a week she would drive to the Johnson Ranch. Wealthy rancher Albert "Stoney" Johnson, a widower with four young children at home, owned 100,000 acres of prime grazing land on the outskirts of

Camp Verde. It was a forty mile drive to the entrance to the ranch.

It was a long drive for Maggie, but Stoney paid her well. Maggie was an 8 to 5 nanny. She would come home exhausted, but still dug deep within herself and found away to take care of her son. Mildred would handle the babysitting chores during the day while Maggie was away. She continued to work on her pottery and her garden when the baby would allow it.

Maggie called the baby, Bucket. After a few years, he became known throughout the county as Maggie's adopted son, Theodore "Bucket" Smith. No one questioned the nickname. The legend of Bucket Smith grew, not because he was left in a bucket on Maggie's doorstep. Instead, the two women were able to keep the secret of the baby's arrival to themselves, but the legend grew anyway thanks to a gift Bucket received from Maggie on his eighth birthday: a basketball.

Bucket took it from there…

Bucket borrowed one of Mildred's tomato barrels, cut a hole in the bottom of it and attached it to a metal pole in the backyard. He shot baskets day and night. He practiced and practiced. He became so good that you could hardly hear the leather ball scrape the barrel. There were times he'd have to replace the barrel, but that was no problem, he'd just rush up to Mildred's and get another one.

He was never without his basketball. On Sundays, Maggie and Mildred would take the young man to church and after the services they'd head to Prescott to sell Mildred's wares. Bucket would always be at their side, following along with that bouncing ball of his. Maggie did draw the line: No basketball in the church pew.

Bucket kept the ball in the car. "Enough is enough," Maggie would say to him.

By the time Bucket entered his middle-school years the basketball had become an extension to his right hand. He was so good that he could dribble around and through the other kids — and some of them on the outdoor courts on the weekends were three, maybe four years older than him. His junior high team never lost a game. Of course, Bucket stood out. The baby in the bucket had grown. At the age of fourteen, Bucket measured six-foot-one inches tall and weighed a shade under 200 pounds.

Of course, it wasn't long before Jules Jones came a calling. Jones was the Cordes Junction High School basketball coach. He was used to winning titles. His teams had won five state titles in the last six years. Jones had been coaching for 30 years and he was just about to announce his retirement when he heard about a tall, burly kid named Bucket, who lived at the edge of the county line.

One day, Jones decided to pay Maggie a visit. The coach never forgot that day. "The Smith place was thirteen miles from town. You had to take Clay Road and head north for a few miles. Then you'd turn on Cherry Farms Road and head east to the last house on the left. The drive was worth it. The first time I saw Bucket, I couldn't believe my eyes," the coach had once said to the Cordes Weekly Examiner. "Bucket was in Maggie's backyard shooting baskets, nailing every shot into a wooden basket. He never missed!"

The following September, Bucket enrolled at Cordes Junction High. Jones took a liking to Bucket. Not because of his basketball skills — although that was an advantage, but simply because Maggie had raised a young man that had the makings of a leader. Jones once said, "He was like a drop in a bucket, he came out of nowhere, plopped down in my office and made an everlasting impression on me." Little did Jones know how close he was to the truth.

Four years later, Bucket would leave school with a diploma and offers to a dozen colleges. He ended up averaging thirty points a game at Cordes High and broke every school record imaginable. Unfortunately his mother had health problems and money was very tight. Mildred had passed on last winter and Bucket needed to do something fast to help out financially. Going away to college wasn't the answer. So, he did what he had to do.

He joined the army.

It was a sad day when Bucket left for boot camp. Thank goodness Maggie had Bucket's high school sweetheart Julia

Childress by her side at the Sky Harbor Airport in Phoenix. Just a few months ago, she had lost her beloved Mildred, and now Bucket would be going away to Vietnam. They had not been apart in 18 years —18 years since she pulled him out of that over-sized metal bucket and held him in her arms.

Maggie would have Julia to comfort her while Bucket was away. After all, they were almost family. Bucket and Julia were engaged to be married. Maggie hugged him and said her final goodbyes. Julia put her arms around Bucket and kissed him. "You come back to us. I love you," she said, as Bucket boarded the plane. The two women watched the airliner take off and soar east over the Superstition Mountains.

It didn't take long for Bucket's body to ache. He needed to stretch those long legs of his. The train rolled on. He looked out the window. The sun was setting. It was time to check out the dinner car. A juicy steak and potatoes sounded good. He wondered if they served such a thing. Within minutes, he had found his way to the dinner car, placed his order and waited for what turned out to be beef and noodles...and a side of salad with some French dressing. Not bad, he thought. It certainly was very different from a New York cut.

Bucket knew one thing for sure. The food in front of him was a lot better than what he had been getting for the last four months in the hospital. Of course, two months before that, he had nothing but IV's and feeding tubes attached to his body.

He stared out the dining car window. His mind took him beyond the tall trees, beyond the lakes and beyond the wide-open countryside that seemed to filter by the window and then disappear into the darkness.

He looked toward the night sky and his thoughts took him to a hospital in Saigon and to a blond nurse, whose warm hands brought him out of a deep sleep, or so it seemed. "Okay, Sergeant Smith, time to eat. I know you're ready for this wonderful hospital food."

Nurse Johansson reached for the lever on the bed. It took a couple of moments before she had the soldier right where she wanted him. "There," she said. "It's great to have you back with us."

Bucket was glad to see Olga. She, along with Dr. Frederick Knowles, were the two most important people in his life the past few months. Without them, he figured he would have had no past and maybe no future. He had come a long way. They had been there for him, night and day. They pulled him through. They gave him his life back and he would never forget them.

Physically, he was fine. As well as could be expected for a man that had been strapped to an operating table with pieces of lead lodged in his right leg, left shoulder and behind his neck.

Yes, he would have scars, both mentally and physically, but he was in one piece. He wished he could say the same for many of the men in his platoon.

"I can't believe you're leaving us tomorrow," Olga said. "I'm going to miss you. I guess it's time for you to go. Time for you to leave us and follow that letter." The nurse pointed to the envelope on the night stand next to the bed.

Bucket picked up the envelope and held it to his chest.

"It's time, Olga. It's time."

"Mommy...Mommy." A young curly haired boy cried out.

The sound of the lad calling for his mother startled Bucket. Within a split second Bucket found himself not in a hospital bed in Saigon, but back on the train, eating dinner and heading for Memphis. He rubbed his eyes, pulled the envelope from his pocket, took out the letter and said, "Julia, I'm on my way."

Bucket shook his head. Two weeks ago he did not know who Julia was. Julia was the final part of the puzzle. His mother was waiting for him in Cordes Junction and so was Julia.

Bucket left the dining car and went back to his seat. Memphis was still a few hours away. He dosed off again and this time he heard a different sound. It was not gunfire, nor an explosion. It was not the soft voice of Nurse Johansson. Nor was it the sounds of the wheels of the train as they clanged against the steel track below.

It was a whistle. A referee's whistle.

"Number 23, you're pushing off...Number 20, blue...you're on the line," roared the man in the black and white stripes. "Son, you're on the line...it's a one and one."

The crowd yelled in unison, "Bucket! Bucket! Bucket!"

The tall boy toed the line. He took one look at the basket and calmly sank the first and then the second free throw. The crowd erupted. The inbounds pass went the length of the court and bounced against the wall as the buzzer sounded, ending the game. The boy they called Bucket was lifted onto the shoulders of his teammates.

The scoreboard read: Cordes Junction 82, Camp Verde 80.

Bucket's teammates lowered him to the floor and the hero bolted into the arms of the blond-haired, smiling cheerleader. He then waved to the crowd, looked down at his sweetheart and said, "Julia, we did it!"

Bucket opened his eyes, The train conductor had put his hand on Bucket's right shoulder. "Hey, soldier. Memphis in twenty minutes."

The Memphis train station still looked the same to Bucket. He threw his duffel bag over his shoulder, looked around the lobby, and eyed a coffee shop, just to the left of the newspaper stand. Six years ago, he had stopped for lunch at the same coffee shop on the way to boot camp. He was a boy then. He was a man now.

Bucket reached into his pocket, pulled out some change and paid the news stand attendant for the daily paper. He found a seat at the counter in the coffee shop and ordered a cup of coffee, two eggs over medium, bacon and toast.

He glanced over the front page of the paper. The headline read: U.S. to send more troops to Vietnam. He stared at the article. He did not need to read past the first paragraph. He glanced around the coffee shop. Three soldiers sat in the corner. He assumed their orders were tucked away in their duffel bags.

A sadness came over him as he turned the stool around and concentrated on the dish of food the waitress had just slid in front of him. He picked up the inside section of the paper and read the headline on the sports page. It read: Texas Western Miners shock Kentucky in NCAA Final.

He read on about an all-black starting five out of El Paso, Texas who shocked the world by beating a heavily favored college basketball team. He thought to himself times have changed. It's about time he thought.

Bucket had spent the last six years, battling to stay alive alongside his fellow soldiers — black, white...no matter the color of their skin, as they fought together for survival in a land far from home. A strange land and certainly very different from the Arizona desert — thousands of miles from the beautiful sunrises and the gorgeous evening sunsets that he was used to.

He didn't understand all the hatred in the world. Why should it matter what color you are? He knew times hadn't changed that much, especially in the South, and especially in places like Memphis where it was common for segregated bathrooms in airports and train stations.

Bucket, shook his head. Hell, it happened in his own state, on the basketball court, before and after a game, at restaurants, at hotels, the hatred was everywhere.

Bucket eyed the black child at the end of the counter. He was putting away a stack of pancakes. His mother, sitting next to him, made sure her child was getting more in his mouth than on the floor.

He would never forget Freddie Greathouse, his friend and starting guard on his high school team. It was an away-game in a small town, near the New Mexico border.

Bucket rubbed his forehead, he couldn't believe he was having breakfast in Memphis and his thoughts had wandered back seven years to Freddie and a come-from-behind win in Solomanville.

Freddie had scored 20 points that night. Bucket recalls it was an off-night for him, just six points, but he did have 14 offensive boards and kept feeding the ball to Freddie. It should have been a night that Freddie would remember for a long time. Instead, after the game the local restaurant forced Freddie to take his burger and fries to the bus. He ate alone.

Freddie remembered the night all right, but for all the wrong reasons.

Bucket came out of his trance. He took a drink of water and signaled the waitress for the bill. He needed to let his thoughts subside for a while. He was getting better at absorbing it all...one minute his thoughts would take him to a foxhole in Vietnam, the next would take him to his teenage days on the basketball court...then to his mother and then to Julia. The puzzle was almost complete. Little did he know, he would return home just in time for another one to begin.

The train ride through western Arkansas, the Texas panhandle, and the dusty, wind-swept terrain of New Mexico seemed long as he fought off muscle spasms and the aches and pains which accompany a man of his size. His body ached and the only exercise he could count on was his trips back and forth to the dining car.

By the time Bucket reached the eastern edge of Arizona, he was ready to jump off the train and hitchhike the rest of the way. He knew he was getting closer...the tumbleweeds bouncing across the desert floor in the early morning light were all he needed to see. He was within five-hundred miles of home. Bucket looked at his watch and quickly checked the time. He was no longer in the Eastern time zone. He was out west and the sun was coming up. Bucket wrestled with his body, trying to find a comfortable position, quickly his thoughts focused on his mother and Julia.

Julia's letters had kept him up to date on his mother's condition. The real kicker came just two weeks before he had entered the foxhole for the final time. The cancer had spread and Doc Wilber Harrison, the Smith's family doctor for more than three decades, had advised Bucket of the progression of his mother's illness through a series of very sad and very short phone conversations.

Bucket stared out the window. He could make out a mountain range, off to the south. He estimated the mountains to be no more than eighty miles away. Beyond those mountains: Mexico. Thousands of miles south of the Sonoran desert was another land, Vietnam. He had finally separated himself from the past. His memory had returned. His future was ahead of him. He needed to get home.

## Chapter 3

Julia panicked. She couldn't find her car keys. She shuffled through the bottom of her purse one more time. The keys were there all the time. She took a deep breath. She had an hour to get to the train station in downtown Phoenix, park her car, and rush to the gate. Bucket was close. He had been gone for so long.

Julia made sure the blanket was snug, giving plenty of warmth to Maggie. She kissed her on the forehead. Maggie was sleeping, peacefully. She left the room, headed downstairs and ran out the front door of Wilhelm Gables. It was a clear day. Blue sky, a little on the warm side, but not hot. Within seconds, she was in her car and heading out of Carefree.

The ride south on I-17 was like being in an Indy 500 race. Julia had learned a long time ago that putting the pedal to the metal wouldn't get her to her destination any faster. Keep at 65 miles per hour and the exits would fly by just the same — Bell Rd., Peoria, Dunlap, Thomas, Indian School...she was getting closer. It seemed like a lifetime ago when she hugged Bucket on the sideline of a Cordes Junction High School basketball game. She was a cheerleader then...she was a woman now. A people person, a business woman, and very good at getting things done.

She ran a hardware store in Cordes Junction. The owner, Stoney Johnson — Maggie's longtime boss and ranch owner, opened the store in 1959 — his third hardware and feed store in the state. He hired Julia, and by the summer of 1960, Stoney handed over the keys and made her the manager of the establishment.

Bucket threw his duffel bag over his shoulder and waited for the crowd to disperse. He could see over everyone. He looked to the left and then to the right, and back to the left...and then he saw her.

"Julia!" he yelled, "Over here...over here!"

Julia rushed to him. Her blond hair bouncing to and fro. "Bucket...Bucket!"

"My soldier boy," she exclaimed, as she rushed into his arms. "You look so handsome."

Within minutes, Bucket and Julia were out of the train station, in Julia's car, and heading north on the interstate to Wilhelm Gables. Bucket listened intently as Julia explained to him the latest on Maggie's condition.

Bucket covered his face with both hands. He tried to hold back the tears. He couldn't, so he let it all out. Julia placed her right hand on his lap. Bucket looked at her and said, "Two weeks...two weeks!"

Julia continued to explain the recent change in Maggie as Bucket stared out the window and watched the exits fly by — Thomas, Dunlap...Bell.

"Julia, your letter. The doctor said a year...maybe two."

"I know, Bucket. I know."

Bucket was angry. He could have been home a week ago. The military transport had broken down in Saigon. To make matters worse the weather forecast wasn't good. His quick decision to take the first commercial flight out to New York and the long train ride home had cost him hours...and days.

"I should have been here sooner."

"You did the best you could, Bucket. You're here now. Your mother will be waking up soon. She's as beautiful as ever. Your mother can't wait to see you," Julia said, as she brushed away her tears with a tissue. "Bucket, you're the strongest man I know...and you need to be even stronger when you walk through the door and into her room."

Bucket looked at Julia and touched her right cheek with his left hand. "I will be, Julia. I will be."

"Maggie...Maggie," Julia said softly, as she sat down in a chair next to the bed and leaned over and touched Maggie's forehead. "Bucket is here. Bucket is here."

"My Bucket," the woman opened her eyes and smiled.

Bucket knelt down and let his mother wrap both arms around him. "Bucket, I've missed you so. I have so much to tell you and there's so little time."

"Mom, please, put your head back on the pillow. I'm here. I'm not going anywhere."

Maggie nodded, her body shaking. She pointed to the closet. "Son, get my jewelry box. You know what it looks like. You made it for me when you were just eleven years old."

Bucket looked at Julia and then he shook his head.

"Okay, Mom, okay."

Before Bucket closed the closet door and turned around, he knew in his heart that his mother was gone. The sound was deafening. It was that dull, long ring of the monitor. He had heard the sound so many times...so many times before at another hospital in another land.

The doctors and the nurses rushed in.

Bucket held the hand-carved jewelry box to his chest. Tears flowed freely as he fell to his knees. Julia rushed to him and held him. She slowly took the box from his hands. She glanced at the four words in dark lettering: To Mom, with Love.

The Cordes Lawn Cemetery sat on a five-acre piece of land, one mile north of town. It was in a secluded area with a lush, green, well-manicured entrance. The area was three hundred feet higher in elevation than the town of Cordes Junction. If you were inclined to sit on one of the numerous benches scattered throughout the complex, you could see Main Street, the Village Square, the Valley National Bank, the sheriff's office and the newly constructed Johnson Library.

The name Johnson was visible everywhere. If you were a passerby or an overnight visitor you would probably assume the town was called Johnsonville.

Stoney Johnson saw to it that Cordes Junction had everything it needed and more. He lent a helping hand to half the residents of Cordes at one time or another.

Bucket was soon to find out that his mother had been at the top of that list.

Maggie was laid to rest along side her friend, Mildred, her partner-in-crime. Bucket and Julia placed the flowers on top of the casket as the two workers continued to lower Maggie into her final resting place. Bucket removed his sunglasses. His eyes were glazed...his pupils red...his face puffy.

The entire town of Cordes Junction was there to pay their respects. Stoney Johnson couldn't bring himself to move closer than one-hundred feet of the ceremony. He stood next to the town sheriff, Joe Arano, and the town's mayor, Roman Walker. The trio, standing together, but alone in their thoughts of Maggie, Bucket...and the past.

Julia and Bucket took the turn off and headed to the Cherry Farms homestead. It had been just 48 hours since the funeral and both of them were still dazed, stunned and not quite themselves, but it was time to focus on Maggie's wishes...time to figure out just what the contents inside the jewelry box meant.

Bucket had opened the box the day before on the porch of Stoney's ranch house. Stoney had gathered all of Maggie's friends, allowing them to pay their final respects to a woman they loved and admired. The sun was setting and a beautiful bright, streaky...orange in color scene had unfolded above the mountains to the west as they sat on Stoney's porch and let the afternoon wind glide by them, as if the wind had the power to clear their thoughts.

Julia sat by Bucket's side as they opened the box and eyed the contents: A set of keys, a will, a deed, a note, and an envelope containing only a piece of paper with what looked to be a license plate number — AZ649-43.

Bucket eyed the setting sun and looked upward. A hand full of stars were barely visible — one twinkled.

"Mother, what is this all about?"

Julia and Bucket stayed at the ranch overnight, but they both slept no more than an hour, or two, if that and now here they where en route to Maggie's place...Bucket's home...Bucket's room...his backyard...his makeshift basketball court...his memories of another life, long before Vietnam.

The Dodge sped toward the house with two very anxious people aboard. A cloud of dust rolled out from underneath the automobile and left a dark colored, tunnel-like trail for 200 feet down the road, finally dissipating — disappearing into the atmosphere.

A giant oak tree covered the entrance to the house on Cherry Farms. The branches reached the edge of the front porch. A wooded fence separated the small, white-framed building from what used to be an open clearing,    located just a few feet away from the eastern edge of the house. The area was all high-grass now and needed Bucket's attention. Somewhere in that pasture was a pole and a tomato bucket. Bucket didn't see either one as he pulled Julia's car into the driveway in front of the house.

"This is home, Julia....our home."

Julia looked at Bucket, touched his face and smiled.

The couple walked around to the back off the house. A wooded gate, wired shut, led to the old rustic barn. A flock of birds were startled by the visitors and flew away to a safer haven.

"The barn is still standing. Needs a lot of work," said Bucket, as he held Julia close to him. They returned to the front of the house and used one of the three keys they had found in the jewelry box.

The living room was just as he had remembered.

A photo of his mom, of Mildred, and of a little boy with a basketball on his lap was the only picture on the eastern wall of the room. The window on the opposite side of the room was covered with a light, tan in color, rolling shade. Bucket raised the shade and looked up the dirt road, which led back to the Clay Road turnoff and the town of Cordes Junction.

Julia and Bucket sat down at the kitchen table. They both took a deep breath and stared at each other. Bucket took out the other two keys from the jewelry box and laid them in the center of the small, oval shaped table — the same table that Bucket sat around years ago and had conversations with his mother about childhood things. The questions seemed important then, especially to a young boy growing up. Now he had 25 years under his belt. His mother was gone. The questions and the answers were about to get harder.

"Julia, the second key is for the cedar chest in mom's room and the other looks like a key to the safe deposit box down at the bank."

"Honey, we can deal with that on Monday, we better take a look in the cedar chest. Your mom's note...she said jewelry box first, cedar chest second and deposit box, third."

Bucket read the note again, it was no more than a few

paragraphs long and signed, "I love you, Bucket...and I am so sorry...please forgive me." The box also contained the deed to the house, and a will leaving the house and all of Maggie's possessions to him, and the small envelope containing a wrinkled piece of paper with a license number.

It was just like his mother to blame herself for leaving him, for dying. Bucket shook his head, she was apologizing. As far as the partial five-digit plate number he had no idea what that was all about.

"Bucket, come here!"

Bucket rushed to the doorway. Julia had taken the second key, gone to the bedroom and had opened the cedar chest. "It's my wedding dress! It's my wedding dress...and there is another note!"

Bucket motioned from the doorway for Julia to read the note.

"She wants us to get married. She wants us to see Judge Crider over at the courthouse and then go see Stoney."

"This is crazy," Bucket said, his voice rattled on. What does

Stoney have to do with this...all of this?"

"It's a beautiful dress," Julia said. "Maggie and Mildred made it for me...for us."

"I know, Julia," Bucket said, trying to smile. His emotions were bouncing around like a basketball. "It's a lovely dress and you know I want to marry you. Why all these steps...the urgency...why is she doing all of this?"

Julia rushed to him and hugged him. It was just too much for him...less than two days since the funeral...and now all this. She had a feeling there was more to come...and so did he.

Julia persuaded him to take a walk with her. "Let's get some air," she said. They went outside and around to the back of the house. They unhooked the gate and made their way to the barn. Parked in the breezeway was Maggie's old Ford pickup. The hood was dusty and the pigeons had left their mark on all the windows.

Bucket opened the passenger side, reached across the seat and fiddled for the keys under the floor mat on the driver's side. He pulled them out. "Right where she's always kept them...she trusted everybody."

"Start it up," Julia said.

So he did. He cracked a smile. "Listen to that engine. I can't believe it turned over."

He turned on the radio and dialed in his favorite channel. It was the Righteous Brothers and 'You've Lost that Loving Feeling'. "This must be a new one, you know these guys?"

"I sure do, honey. I listen to them all the time."

So much time lost, he thought, as he listened to the tune.

Bucket turned off the radio and the engine. He took a quick look under the hood and then closed it. He softly rolled his right hand over the hood. "Well, Julia. We have a house and a pickup. It's what mother wanted. Her tactics are a mystery, but tomorrow we'll make some calls, see Judge Crider then we'll take this old Ford out to Stoney's and get some answers."

"Bucket are you sure," Julia said. "My head is swimming. Are you thinking clearly?"

"We've waited too long. Whatever mother has in store for us down the road. She's right about one thing, we need to do this, together."

Bucket and Julie wrapped their arms around each other. In the back of their minds, they knew Maggie had something in store for them...something that they both needed to do together.

The wedding may not happen tomorrow, but soon. Maggie

would get her wish...it may take a couple of weeks longer than his mother had wanted, but Bucket would honor his mother's wishes — all of them.

Judge Samuel Crider had aged some.

Bucket remembers being in his office many years ago, tagging along with his mother, with his basketball close to his side. Crider was a lawyer then. He had certainly moved up in the world, at least in the small town of Cordes Junction. Bucket figured Crider must have been in his late 40s then...and now, he must be pushing 60...maybe 61 with a bald head and some bushy eyebrows under that Arizona State University football cap that he loved to wear, daily.

"Come on in, you two. I've been expecting you."

Julia and Bucket walked into the chambers and sat down next to each other on a leather sofa near Judge Criner's desk.

"Bucket, I'm so sorry to hear about your mother," Judge Crider said. "But I'm pleased to see you back from that ugly war and in one piece."

"Thank you, Judge. I'm not sure I'm in one piece, but I seem to be on the mend. It's such a shocker with my mother gone. I guess we knew it was coming, but I thought we'd have more time...enough time to do things together...catch up on all those lost years. I feel so robbed of that."

"I know, Bucket, I know," the Judge said, sadly.

Bucket grabbed Julia's hand. She sat quietly. They both looked around the chambers and Bucket blurted out, "Why are we here, Judge?"

"Awe yes," Judge Criner said. Your mother's wishes."

Judge Crider reached for the folder on his desk. "In here is the marriage license, just need a couple of signatures and I'll take care of the rest. I'm sure you've gone through the jewelry box by now. Oh, how she loved that box. She's specific on what you two are to do next. So, I'll keep my mouth shut and send you out to Stoney's place."

"But...Judge Crider!"

"Sorry, Bucket. I'll handle all this legal stuff. We'll go over it all in good time. You two head on out and see Stoney."

Bucket was beside himself, but relented. "Okay, Judge, okay."

It had been eight years since Bucket had been out to Stoney's ranch. He had always enjoyed the trip. His mother would gas up the pickup on a Saturday morning and the two of them would head north toward Camp Verde. Of course, his mother made the drive everyday for years, but occasionally she'd surprise

Bucket and say to him, "Grab that old bamboo pole out in the barn...get some worms out of the compose pile and let's head up to Stoney's place."

Sometimes, if he was lucky, they'd stay the weekend. He'd get to sleep in the bunkhouse, stay up late and listen to the ranch hands discuss everything from cows and horses, to branding, and lassoing...and probably a few things a young boy shouldn't hear.

On this afternoon, with Julia next to him, he drove down the highway emotionally spent. The words of the song, blaring out of the radio sounded familiar. He had heard the tune a few days ago at the little cafe at the train station in Memphis. The voice of Percy Sledge...the song: *When a Man Loves a Woman*.

He looked over at Julia. She was so beautiful. He had had very little time to tell her so, or discuss such things. They would build a life together...she would look so lovely in her wedding dress. Julia would have her wedding, but something was wrong he could feel it. It had nothing to do with Julia...that uneasy feeling...that pain in his chest had nothing to do with his injuries from the war, but something else...something down the road...30 miles away. Stoney had the answers to all his questions...he could feel it.

The entrance to the ranch was just ahead, the area reminded Bucket of a scene from an old Gene Autry television series. When he was a wide-eyed, innocent child, he used to sit in front of the black and white RCA television and watch Autry ride through the desert, chasing bad guys in black hats. Looking back on it now, he realized how simple life was then...and could there have been that many bad guys to contend with, every week?

Bucket shook his head. His mind was wandering as he took his right foot off the pedal, slowed the car down, pulled in behind the slow-moving 16-wheeler ahead of him, and awaited the entrance to the ranch.

"Bucket, are you...okay?" Julia said, as she watched him make the right turn off the highway and maneuver his way over the cattle guard and through the open gate. She could see both his hands clutching the steering wheel so hard that his fingers were turning red.

"I'm all right, honey. I was in another place for a moment. I'm fine," he said, as the automobile rambled on, leaving in its wake the vibration below. A sign shook on the fence post as they crossed the cattle guard. It read: property of Stoney Johnson, no hunting, no fishing without permission from Johnson Properties.

Stoney stood on the porch. He had just given instruction to four of his cowhands and as they dispersed he looked up the road.

He knew it was Bucket and Julia. The time had come.

Bucket and Julia got out of the car slowly and made their way to the ranch house. Bucket would never forget Stoney's porch, it circled around the entire first floor of the three-story structure.

One hot, summer afternoon, many years ago, Bucket circled the porch a dozen times, after being stung by a wasp. He remembers his mother, and Stoney, and a couple of ranch hands ignoring him. They all thought he was playing a game of 'Cowboys and Indians'. Instead, he was putting his hand to his mouth, yelling, in pain, as the unwanted insect had planted its stinger onto his upper lip.

"Hello, Bucket...Julia," Stoney said, as he stepped off the porch and hugged Julia and shook hands with Bucket.

"Boy, Bucket, you're looking more like country folk with those jeans on, a T-shirt and that John Deere hat from... I bet that hat is from Lyle Crandall's old clothing store over on Sycamore Street."

Bucket, realizing he had normal attire on for the first time since his return, took off the hat, eyed the brim.

"You know, you're right. Mom got this hat for me when I was thirteen."

"That's a great hat. You know old man Crandall owned that clothing store for more than 20 years. He closed down last spring." Stoney said. "He couldn't compete with Randall Lewiston anymore. That man has things pretty well wrapped up with stores in Camp Verde, Prescott and North Phoenix."

Stoney scratched his chin.

"Last I heard, Lyle moved to Tucson to be near his daughter, She owns a bed-and-breakfast in the foothills, near the Catalina Mountains. A beautiful place. I've been there a couple of times."

Bucket shook his head. "Stoney, you still get around, don't you?"

"Yeah, Bucket, I try to keep busy. I'll be seventy-two next month. I'm afraid if I slow down, this old arthritis will get the best of me." Stoney flexed his fingers on his left hand. "I don't do much calf roping anymore."

There was a moment of silence. It was as if the three of them knew it was time for the small talk to end...and time for Bucket and Julia to get some answers.

Stoney cleared his throat.

"I want you two to take a ride with me," Stoney said, as he took a deep breath and pointed to his Willys Jeep. The Jeep was parked next to the corral where two ranch hands were hard at work unloading the flatbed of a semi truck full of hay.

Stoney took Bucket and Julia down the dusty road.

Bucket had been on the road before. He knew after a few twists and turns the road would come to an end at the closest of the six ponds on the ranch. Bucket thought back. His mother had sat with him on a picnic table at the edge of that pond. Tears were streaming down her cheeks. He was maybe eight or nine years old at the time.

Bucket remembers the exact words his mother had uttered that day. She had said to him, "I can't tell you Bucket...I can't tell you."

Those words were already pounding in his ears, over and over again, as Stoney made a swift turn and drove the Jeep the final few yards through a meadow and finally into a u-shaped bend in the road.

The picnic table was still there.

The three of them got out of the Jeep and headed for the table. Bucket reached the cemented table first and he ran his right hand across the surface, his fingertips edging closer and finally stopping on the carved initials — TS and MS. Six months ago, he couldn't remember one moment of his past...and now he remembers, everything.

The three of them sat down on the picnic table and eyed the clear blue surface of the water. They looked north across the pond and took in the breathtaking view of the purple mountains far off in the distance.

"You're going to tell me about my father, Herman Smith, aren't you, Stoney?"

"We can begin there, Bucket. We can begin there."

Stoney looked up at the sky.

He warned Julia and Bucket that he had so much to tell them, but the late afternoon wind gust would make it uncomfortable to stay very long. The surface of the water was already showing ripples, which were becoming miniature waves as they rolled to and fro from the southern edge of the pond all the way to the northern end.

He was stalling, but he also knew the trip to the pond would help Bucket in the long run. He was right. He could see it in the young man's eyes. The picnic table, the pond, the meadow, the view of the mountains — all of it would be good for Bucket. This was just Step 1 of the process. It would be a long day...and a long night for all three of them.

He explained to Bucket and Julia that Alexandra was making dinner and it would be better if he could continue their talk, after dinner, in the privacy of his den.

Julia nodded. Bucket agreed. Julia knew Alexandra. In fact she had sat in the front row of the

Methodist Church in Cordes last summer and watched the couple recite their wedding vows. Bucket, of course, would be meeting Alexandra for the first time.

The Johnson marriage had been a surprise to everyone in town, except for Stoney and Alexandra, that is. The two met a year ago February at the Prescott Rodeo. They have been inseparable ever since. The fact Alexandra was twelve years younger, Italian, and a little stubborn didn't seem to matter to Stoney. After all, Stoney had a stubborn streak as well. They kind of mirrored each other in that regard and whatever flaws they had, well they seemed to work around them.

On the ride back to the ranch, Bucket squeezed Julia's hand. He wasn't sure he wanted Stoney to rehash the past if it involved his father, Herman Smith. He knew enough about the man, mostly from listening to Aunt Mildred and his mother talk about him at the kitchen table — just once, as he, at the age of seven — maybe eight, hid in the hallway with his left ear pushed against the wall. They were whispering and he didn't catch all the conversation, but his young ears had heard enough.

The man had left them. That was all he needed to know. His father had left him and his mother to fend for themselves. He never secretly hid in the hallway ever again. He had heard enough...and even now, he remembers the pain in his mother's voice, as she mentioned the name of Herman Smith to Aunt Mildred, on that afternoon as the two women sipped on ice tea and discussed adult things.

He recalls putting both hands over his ears and quickly running out the back door, into the barn, up the steps of the ladder and into the far corner of the hayloft...hiding behind the biggest bale of hay he could find.

Theodore "Bucket" Smith discovered early on that things were a little different down on Cherry Farms Road. Sure, the other boys and girls in Cordes Junction had a mother and a father, but they didn't have the best mom in the world, they didn't have a Maggie Smith... nor did they have an Aunt Mildred.

He decided on that day in the dark corner of the barn, while listening to the sounds of the pigeons — cooing in the rafters, that the two women, sitting at the kitchen table, sipping on their tea, would make him feel safe. He didn't need a father. He didn't need a man called Herman Smith.

Stoney's den looked the same to Bucket as it had years ago when he used to jump around on the huge leather sofa and get dirty looks from his mother. The Elk head, above the fireplace, couldn't be ignored. It was the biggest rack of antlers Bucket had ever seen as a little boy...and still. On the northern wall of the den was a glass case containing the map of the Johnson Ranch.

Bucket and Julia sat on the sofa while Stoney and Alexandra sat in the matching dark brown leather chairs -- one located on one side of the fireplace and the other centered on the south side of the room. Beautiful hand-woven rugs covered the wooded floor. A mahogany desk with a black top and a matching swivel chair were located in the western end of the room.

"That was a great dinner, Alex," Julia said.

"Yes, it was," Bucket added, as he stared at the beautiful Alexandra Johnson, trying to put the two of them — Stoney and Alexandra, together as a couple. The two were definitely in love with each other. Bucket could tell that right off.

Stoney smiled at his wife. "Alex, why don't you show Julia your latest artwork." He then glanced back over at Bucket.

The two women headed for the doorway. Alexandra stopped and listened to Stoney carry on.

"Bucket, she's something else. We met at the Prescott Rodeo. She was doing a portrait of an old cowboy, who just an hour before had been knocked off a bronc. He might have lasted six seconds...the sketch took about an hour and a half. Alex would have finished the sketch sooner, but I came along with my two left feet and knocked over the painting."

"That's exactly how we met and he is still stumbling around," Alex said, jokingly. "Come on Julia, I want to show you what we did to the girls' rooms, too. My studio is across the hall."

The girls, Judy and Katherine Anne, were the only children left at home...and they were no longer children. Judy was sixteen and Katherine Anne would be seventeen in just three days. The boys, Jacob and Stoney, Jr. were in college — Jacob at Michigan State and Stoney, Jr., was closer to home in his senior year at Northern Arizona University.

Bucket remembered Judy and Katherine Anne. Both Johnson girls chased him all over the confines, in and around, the ranch house. The girls older brothers were in middle school or just getting out of elementary school when he was a senior in high school. Bucket couldn't remember all their ages, but one thing was for sure...his mother had a hand in raising all of them.

With Alex and Julia out of the room, Stoney headed for the fireplace and grabbed a 5X7 photo off the mantel.

"Bucket, here's a photo of all my kids, you, and Maggie. "There was never a dull moment back then. You kids were always in and out of trouble."

Stoney placed the picture back on the mantel and headed for his desk. Bucket saw him take something out of the middle drawer. It was another photo. Stoney handed the picture to Bucket, took a deep breath and said, "This is a picture of me...and Maggie...and Herman Smith."

Bucket squirmed in his seat as he listened to each word out of Stoney's mouth.

Stoney cleared his throat, took a deep breath and said, "Herman Smith always felt like he was swimming up stream.

To him life was a journey all right. The trouble was he was

always going one way and everyone else was headed in the opposite direction. He didn't plan it that way, it just happened. As a child, growing up on the outskirts of Los Angeles in the 1920s, he was left alone a lot.

Herman's parents were both gamblers. Horse racing, card playing...they went where the money was. They couldn't survive like normal folk, no that was just too hard, instead, they hustled in and out of smoky, dark card rooms, dusty race tracks—scheming and conniving their way through life, involved in one illegal activity after another.

There were good times. He used to come home from school and find a present or two on his bed, or they'd spend a day at the park, or zoo, or the three of them would spend a lazy Sunday afternoon on the beach. Those times were rare and those times occurred only when his parents were on a winning streak and were rolling in the dough.

When things were going bad, his parents would argue, throw things and curse at each other. Herman would grab his coat, run out the back door, hit the streets and look for trouble.

The young Smith was always in trouble with the local police—shoplifting, throwing rocks through the windows of businesses, you name it, chances are Herman was involved in it—all the things a young boy, left unattended, could get involved in.

The only skill he learned as a young teenager was playing cards. He could shuffle, and deal, and take cash from an unsuspecting novice player to a professional card shark. Sometimes he'd win, get beat up, thrown in an alley by much older men, and sometimes, more often than naught, he'd walk around whatever town he'd happen to be in with a lot of money in his pocket — acting like he didn't have a care in the world.

His parents had taught him plenty. He was street smart, tough...a survivor.

Herman left Los Angeles just a few months after his parents were killed in a rollover accident along the coastal highway near Long Beach. Photos of the accident made the front page in all the LA papers. Herman really felt alone in the world after that, but then again, he was used to it. Leaving town was no problem.

Money was not a problem. To his surprise, his parents had taken out an accidental death insurance policy and as it turned out, he was the recipient. Add to that his poker winnings, and that left him with enough cash to keep himself adrift in the gambling world. At least for a few years, that is.

He decided to set up shop in Prescott. His new home: the Palace Bar on Whiskey Row. He picked up a day job as a used car salesman at O'Reilly Motors and to his surprise held on to the gig for quite a while. He became very good at it and even worked his way up to assistant manager. He'd drive around town in a late-model Ford or Chevy. Of course, the cars were not his...they were all owned by the dealership but that didn't matter, the residents of Prescott didn't know that. The man behind the wheel looked successful and in the long run his showmanship probably aided in a sale or two.

The young poker-playing, sales executive was good-looking, personable, and he had a knack for reading the minds of his victims. He could close the deal with a customer, sending them out of the dealership smiling from ear to ear or sit across from them in a poker game and take their money.

More often than naught, Herman would lean back in his chair at the Palace Bar and stare at the poker player across from him. The man would lower the brim of his Stetson, shade his eyes, take a puff on his cigar and nudge his bet toward the center of the table. The man figured he had the goods on the young man with the pleasant smile.

Herman would let out a big grin and simply say, raise.

Chances are the old poker player would take the cigar out of his mouth, take a deep sigh and throw his cards into the center of the pot.

If the man only knew that Herman was holding Ace High. Absolutely...nothing.

Of course, Herman realized that someday, if he didn't change his ways, he would end up just like the old fellow with the cigar. But, Herman was a little different from most when it came to poker. He loved winning but he always felt bad about taking their money. He never quite put a handle on why he felt that way, but he did.

It wasn't that he was embarrassed about letting the outside world know that he made his living playing cards. In fact, it wasn't really a deep concern of his, until he went to a Prescott rodeo dance on a Saturday night in February of 1938.

Maggie Haggerty changed his way of thinking...at least temporarily."

Bucket held the photo for a moment and then handed it back to Stoney. He shrugged his shoulders and sat back down.

It was hard for Stoney to continue to get the words out. Of course, he looked across the room and knew the young man was in for a long night and the tale of Herman Smith was just the tip of the iceberg.

Stoney explained to Bucket that he had met Maggie and Herman in the late 1930s in Prescott. "Don't hold me to the date. I'm getting older and my memory is not what it used to be." Stoney looked at the back of the photo. "I guess it was 1938. Alice, bless her heart, could have told you the day, the time and the days leading up to it... and after, for that matter."

Bucket remembered Alice. She was always pinching his cheeks and giving him big hugs, every time his mother brought him out to the ranch for a visit.

Alice kept Stoney on a short leash. Bucket did recall that. Stoney took care of the ranch, but Alice was the boss once he walked through the ranch house door and threw his Stetson on the hat rack.

Alice passed away from an unknown virus, just two years

after the Johnson's fourth child was born. It was a sad time — his mother had told him. Many of the residents of Cordes Junction rallied behind Stoney, and gave him all the support they could, during those agonizing months following her untimely death.

Bucket knew for a fact that Stoney Johnson had repaid the townsfolk tenfold.

The rancher quickly let his thoughts of Alice subside as he continued to clue Bucket in on the saga of Maggie and Herman.

"It was at a dance hall on the outskirts of town. The two of them kinda reminded me of another young couple — a redheaded, full of vinegar cowgirl by the name of Alice and a stubborn, and clumsy, know-it-all rancher with an SJ on his belt buckle. Herman and Maggie fell for each other...just like we did."

Bucket listened intently as Stoney recalled losing sight of the young couple after the Prescott rodeo dance, but ran into them on Main Street in Cordes Junction a few months later.

I had heard that Herman had become a professional card player and spent a lot of time in Prescott at the tables. He must have been good at it...he always had money in his pocket...and at one time had enough money to go in with Maggie and buy those forty acres over on Cherry Farms Rd. It was a great, little place. A little white house with a big red barn...certainly big enough for a couple...and maybe a kid, or two. Stoney stopped talking for a second, looked at Bucket and said, "I guess you know all about Cherry Farms...I'm not telling you anything new, there."

Stoney said there were many rumors going around that Herman was spending too much time away from home — especially at night. "Herman didn't come right out and say to Maggie the reason he was leaving her was because he was drawn to the poker tables, no he probably came up with another excuse for leaving, an excuse that would satisfy him and make more sense to Maggie. At any rate, a year later he was gone."

"Oh, I think he loved Maggie all right. But the thirst for the poker tables was something he had grown up with. He wanted to change. I think he had in his mind that he could leave that life behind. He couldn't pull it off. His addiction to cards won out."

Stoney paused, picked up the glass of water that was on the table and took a swig.

"I'll never get over what he did to my mother," Bucket said. "It's weird that I can't remember a thing about him. I must have been a baby. My mother wouldn't talk about him...the only bits and pieces of information I got...was one time when I overheard a conversation between my mother and Mildred.

Stoney sighed. "Let's talk about Maggie."

Bucket still had plenty of questions about Herman Smith, but he allowed Stoney to continue.

As Stoney continued, Bucket began to realize how little he knew about his mother's early years. He realized the most important person in her life — was him.

Bucket didn't know at that precise moment that the man sitting across from him, wanted him to know that particular fact...and much more. The rancher had seen a lot in his seventy-plus years, but he also knew that Bucket, even at twenty-five, had been through a lifetime of pain, most of that pain caused not from an upbringing in Cordes Junction — that would turn out to be the good times, but the pain in the young man's gut was from another land, in a place where the older of the two men couldn't even begin to imagine.

Bucket knew his mother was from Tennessee. She was very smart, graduated from high school in just three years...at the top of her class. She was beautiful, full of life and was alone in Cordes Junction — at least, in the beginning.

Stoney talked fast. He was quickly filling in the blanks.

Maggie's parents had passed on — first her father, when she was just sixteen, and her mother, a year later. Her father was a heavy smoker.

Her father died in his mid-50s. Maggie's mother died of natural causes. She just passed away on a Sunday morning while her daughter was outside on the porch, dressed for church, waiting patiently for her mother to bring the car around.

Six months later Maggie boarded a bus and headed for Arizona in hopes of starting a new life. She didn't know what to expect. For all she knew there were Cowboys and Indians at every corner. That, of course, was not the case.

She didn't feel comfortable in Phoenix. The town seemed too big for her — ten, maybe twenty times the size of her hometown back in Andersonville, Tennessee.

Instead, she settled in Cordes Junction. The town seemed more like her hometown. She answered an ad in the Cordes Examiner and took a job at Walden's Drugstore. She had saved her money, and deposited the funds she had received from selling her parent's place in Andersonville.

Maggie rented a small, one bedroom apartment on Second Street. It even had a white, picket fence with a small...maybe 20-foot long section of grass, located just to the left of the sidewalk, and another 10 feet or so along the east-side. It came furnished. Her first purchase, other than the essentials — a used push mower from Crandall's hardware store.

Maggie kept busy and things were going well. She loved to dance — especially the Jitterbug, a dance she had learned from her mother early in life. Dancing the Jitterbug is not something you do alone. So, on Friday nights she'd join the so-called "wild group" in town and spent hour after hour dancing the night away at Sonny's Hideout, a bar and grill located just south of town at the end of Clay Road.

Eventually, it wasn't the nights at Sonny's that got her in

trouble, but it was the Saturday night jaunts to Prescott. It was there she met Herman Smith. Upon their first meeting, he said to her, "I can't dance." He lied.

A few months later, they were married at the Cordes Junction courthouse. Judge Criner did the honors. The Judge's wife, Greta, witnessed the ceremony. As usual a handful of photos were snapped by a court beat reporter by the name of Ricky Jackson.

Bucket was hearing all of this for the first time. Of course and there was plenty more to come.

Stoney had taken a moment. There was a small icebox in the corner of the den. He reached in and grabbed two bottles of beer. He opened the bottles and handed one to Bucket.

"I hired your mom...I'd say it must have been just after she quit her job at the drugstore and not long after Herman had left. She needed more money and I needed a nanny in the worst way."

"One Saturday afternoon...."

Stoney had reached down within himself and let out some

air, which had been storing up inside of him.

"Maggie had taken you out to the pond...you know the pond we just came from. When you came back, Alice took you and the kids horseback riding. Maggie was crying, she sat right where you're sitting."

Bucket remembered all right. It was the second time today that he had relived the agony...the feeling of that moment when his mother had been so upset.

He was about to find out why. Bucket knew the next words out of Stoney's mouth would not be good. He could feel it. He wanted to hear all of it...yet, he was now very afraid.

Stoney got up, went to the door way, and yelled. "Alex, could you send Julia in."

Bucket heard the commotion as both women made their way down the spiral staircase. Alex took her right hand and held Julia's hands...and then gave the young girl a concerned look...smiled, and headed off to the kitchen.

Julia sat next to Bucket. They both waited.

"It was June 1941, and Maggie had just taken her laundry basket..."

Bucket and Julia were frozen, stunned, shocked and unable to move as Stoney's words echoed off the walls of the den. Bucket expected to hear a strange tale, especially after all that had happened in the last forty-eight hours. He had hoped Stoney would be able to answer all his questions, wrap everything up in a big bow and hand it to him. Over and done with.

Instead, his life...the past he had fought so hard to regain memory of...now shattered. His battle to stay alive...for what? For a lie!

Stoney and Julia rushed to the window. Bucket was gone.

Julia and Stoney listened as the sound of the grandfather clock signaled the top of the hour. Julia realized the old freestanding antique clock in the corner of Stoney's living room had rung three times since Bucket had rushed out of the ranch house.

"Stoney, shouldn't we go after him?" "No, Julia. I know where he's at. I just talked to Sheriff Arano." "Sheriff Arano!" Julia shouted. "He knows about this?"

"Yes, Joe knows. So does Judge Criner."

"My, God! How did Maggie...how did all of you keep this a secret?"

Stoney explained it was Maggie's secret. "She had stayed true to her story for years, along with Mildred...God rest her soul...God rest both of them. It wasn't until Bucket was grade school age, when she could no longer keep going with her make-up story that Bucket was the child of her cousin, Belle, from Tennessee. Of course there was no cousin Belle. The story worked and the townsfolk bought into it...and after a while, I think the two women believed their own story."

Stoney looked out the window and stared up the road. "He's at Maggie's...I mean Cherry Farms...I mean Bucket is there. He's parked in front of the house. Joe will keep an eye on him. He's got to be going through..."

"Stoney, Bucket is never going to get a handle on this. This is too much. Nobody should have to go through this."

"Bucket will get through it and he'll come back to you. He's going to need you...all of us. When he's ready, we'll be there for him."

"My, God. Stoney, you're going to be there? Help us, whatever it takes, aren't you?"

"Yes, I signed on...forever. I'm Bucket's godfather."

Bucket got up from the kitchen table, opened the cupboard over the sink, and reached for the matches. He had to lash out at something or someone.

He yelled out for Joey and unleashed all his ammo...he didn't stop...he didn't hear the click, nor did he realize the shell casings were no longer falling into the muddy surface below his feet.

He rubbed his eyes and realized he was at Cherry Farms, in the living room...staring at a photo of a little boy with a basketball in his hand. A lovely, slender woman to the left of the boy, an older woman to the right.

Bucket got up, walked outside, down the steps, and headed for the field.

The small area east of the house burned quickly. The fire subsided. Only a layer of smoke was visible, swirling, high above the old oak tree, heading in a westerly direction, moving directly over the head of Sheriff Arona, who stood next to his police car...and waited.

"Wanda, don't send the fire truck, copy?"

"Copy!" the female voice echoed through Joe's radio. "Over and out."

Sheriff Arona started up his vehicle and edged closer to the house. He could see Bucket, standing in the center of the field, eyeing the rubble at his feet. It was what was left of a wired tomato basket and a pole...covered with ashes and smoldering.

"Are you okay, Bucket?"

"I'm okay, Joe." Bucket responded. "I'm okay."

It was as if Bucket knew the sheriff was watching over him. His response was soft spoken. Even in his emotional state, Bucket was aware of his surroundings. His military training had seen to that.

Arona could sense the soldier's awareness right off. He could sense the strength of the young man. He knew Bucket had been bombarded not with bullets over the last forty-eight to seventy-two hours, instead, he had dealt with an emotional trauma with the loss of his mother...the lies that followed her to her grave, the mystery surrounding it all, and the powers-to-be in the small town of Cordes Junction that ultimately would fill in the blanks and help him get his life back on track.

"Bucket, we need to get your hand looked at."

Arona surveyed the field. The fire had done little damage and Bucket's hand would be fine. Twenty minutes at the emergency room would take care of it.

The two men watched as the fire burned out and the smoke settled. "Joe, would you call Julia?"

"Done."

# Chapter 4

The clerk handed the keys to Room 203 to the man who walked with a limp. "It's upstairs and to your right. You will at least have a good view of our town."

"Thank you sir," said the tall, slender and slightly gray-haired man. "You've been very kind."

Hotel Cordes was the oldest inn in town. Most of the visitors passing through town stayed out near the interstate. There were three motels just off the highway and all three came with more up to date accommodations.

There was nothing wrong with Hotel Cordes. It was clean and well kept and Wilbur Hopkins has been a clerk at the establishment for a good twenty years. Hopkins received his check on the first of every month and the check came from Johnson Properties, so he was well aware he worked for Stoney Johnson.

Hopkins watched the man push the elevator button, lean on his cane and waited for the door to open.

"It takes a little time but it'll be down soon," said the clerk, as he motioned upward with his pen in his right hand.

The elevator opened and the new passenger entered and allowed the door to close. Hopkins shook his head and said, "See, I told you so." The hotel clerk looked down at his ledger and muttered, "that man looks familiar."

Herman Smith surveyed his new room. A queen-sized bed, a television, a circular table with two chairs, a bathroom with a shower and one dresser. That about covered it, he thought. He opened the curtain and opened the sliding glass door which lcd to a small patio with a wrought iron table and two chairs.

He sat down for a moment and took in the view of the town of Cordes Junction. Off in the distance he could see the cemetery, Maggie's final resting place. A tear rolled down his face. He uttered in a low voice, "I'm so sorry, Maggie."

Herman had parked on a ridge near the cemetery and witnessed Maggie's funeral. He had wanted to walk down there, pull Bucket aside, and tell him how sorry he was about the loss of his mother. He wanted to release all the guilt he was feeling and fill in the blanks for the young man who was not only grieving over the loss of Maggie but was in agony with more question than answers.

Herman was on the run. When wasn't he? He couldn't make himself leave town. He had stayed up all night. He drove and drove. Finally, he pulled off to the side of the road. When was this going to stop? When the sun came up, he stopped at an all-night diner in

Mayer, ate breakfast, left the eatery and got in his car.

He turned on the ignition and pulled up to the highway. If he turned left, he could head to Las Vegas and then maybe on to Oregon or Washington. It didn't really matter. He could turn right head to Cordes Junction and ease the pain of a young man whose life was in shambles.

Herman turned right and thirty minutes later checked into Hotel Cordes, unsure, afraid...and with no idea of what to do next.

Herman laid down on the bed. He was tired. He was always tired... tired or running, tired of living a lie, tired of looking over his shoulder. He fell asleep and the nightmare began again.

How would he explain to the young man where it all went wrong? Leaving Maggie was the worst decision he ever made. The poker tables led to his destruction. Oh, for a while he lived the high-life with a winning streak which would carry him from the back room tables in the bars along Whiskey Row in Prescott to the seedy tables in LA and finally to Las Vegas and the big time where thousands could be won or lost in just one hand.

He made a name for himself in Las Vegas. He was so good at his profession that sponsors came a calling. Sponsors who would stake him — give him all the money he would need to keep in the GAME. The kicker: Herman would pay the donors back and then some.

The sponsors were members of a Mafia organization who ran the streets of Las Vegas. If you tried to pull a fast one on them, you were history. Herman crossed them once, and that was enough to send him into a tailspin and a life on the run.

And if things weren't bad enough. He wasn't alone. He had befriended a female dealer by day, a card shark by night. Together they worked for the organization.

The two fell in love. They were certainly two peas in a pod. Flame Flattery was a beautiful redhead and if you were unlucky enough to be playing at her table, chances are you were watching her and not the cards in your hand.

The decision to take their money and run was Flame's. There certainly was enough to start a new life in another city, another state...another casino some where far away from Las Vegas. So, Herman went along with the idea and they made their getaway and headed for the Coast of California.

A year went by without a hitch. He got a job selling cars in downtown LA. The money wasn't coming in fast enough and Flame was pregnant. So, he found himself in a couple of easy-to-get-into games against some novice players on the south side of LA.

He got on a winning-streak. Things were looking up and Flame gave birth on a beautiful spring day in mid-April to an eight-pound, 10 ounce boy.

Two months later, the couple's past caught up with them.

Herman saw the door knob turn and the next forty-seconds flashed by quickly. Still, to this day, those seconds are so embedded in his mind.

Herman reached for his revolver, but the taller of the two

men got off a shot and the bullet hit Flame just below her right ear. Blood spattered on the apartment wall as Herman rolled off the bed and fired two shots — one hit the tall man right between the eyes, the other caught the smaller figure square in the chest.

Herman heard the cry of his son. He rushed into the baby's bedroom, picked up the child and held him tightly. Flame was dead. Herman glanced at the clock. It was midnight. The streets were clear.

He knelt down beside Flame. "Oh, my God," he cried out. He

grabbed the car keys, covered the baby with a blanket, rushed down the stairs, got in his car and he was gone.

Hopkins sat in the back room, agonizing over where he had seen the gentleman in Room 203 before. Hopkins was a hotel clerk by day and somewhat of a town historian by night. In fact, he collected just about every newspaper article concerning the town of Cordes Junction.

He had an inclination that somewhere in those many albums of his would be a clue on just who the man in 203 really is.

He was right.

After an hour of shuffling through page after page of articles, Hopkins came across a wedding photo and a caption which read: Herman Smith from Prescott and Maggie Haggerty, a resident of Cordes Junction, were married today at the Courthouse in front of the Honorable Judge Criner. Witnesses included Greta Criner, Joe Arano and Mayor Walker.

"I knew it," Hopkins said out loud. He reached for the phone, looked up the number and dialed his boss, Stoney Johnson.

Herman had fought off another nightmare and somehow with the help of a bottle of Jim Beam fell back to sleep.

He was startled by a knock at the door. He looked out the sliding glass door. He must have slept all afternoon. He jumped up, reached for his revolver and quickly made his way to the door.

"Who is it?" Herman shouted, clutching the gun high above his head.

"It's Stoney Johnson. Please Herman, let me in."

"Stoney, what are you doing here?"

"I'm here to help you, Herman. I'm here to help you. Open the door."

Herman reached for the lock, pushed it down and Stoney entered the room.

"Why are you back here, Herman? You've picked a great day to make an entrance."

"I can't run anymore, Stoney. I need to set the record straight. Pay my respects to Maggie and ease the pain of a young man who must be going through hell."

"My, God. Bucket has enough on his mind today without you showing up."

"Stoney I have to come clean. My days are numbered. It's time, Stoney, it's time."

"Grab your stuff. Let's get you checked out of here and out to the ranch. Whatever you need to say to Bucket, you need to do it now. I will set up the meeting."

# Chapter 5

Herman followed closely behind Stoney's Cadillac. His eyes were fixated on the license plate ahead of him which read: Stoney 1. Herman tried his best to stay within fifty feet of Stoney's vehicle.

The two cars pulled off the interstate, rolled through the gate and on to Stoney's property. The license plate on Herman's vehicle read: AZ 649-43.

Stoney rushed Herman into the den.

Stoney was beside himself. Twenty-four hours ago Bucket sat where Herman is sitting now. "My, God. You look like you need some food in that belly of yours. I'll get Alexandra to make us some sandwiches. You sit tight I'll be right back."

Herman looked around Stoney's den. How can one man have so much and another so little? Choices, he thought. Stoney made all the right moves...made all the right turns on a road to a happy life.

Herman knew he had made the wrong turns...over and over again. He had followed a crooked road and it had led to nothing but destruction. His lies were going to end soon and the sooner the better. The clock was ticking. He could feel it. All the agony for everyone would be over soon.

Stoney returned to the den, along with Alexandra and enough food to fill a whole bunkhouse full of Stoney's cowhands.

Herman was hungry, but he would need more than a couple of sandwiches and a shot or two of

Stoney's whiskey to give him the strength needed to come clean to his son.

"Stoney, I've been on the run so long. I don't know where to begin," Herman said, as he looked into the face of the only man he knew who could possibly guide him through this and help him find a way to ease the pain of his son.

"Her name was Flame. We met in Las Vegas. We both had found our way into the sleazy underworld of The Strip…"

Stoney sat motionless.

Earlier in the day, he had convinced Bucket that Herman Smith was not his father. He had shattered the life of the young man who had been bombarded with the shock of his life when he learned the woman he just buried wasn't his mother...and that his father wasn't his father.

Stoney reached for the phone. Herman sat quietly with his head lowered. He felt like he had just lifted a 200-pound barbell off his shoulder. He listened to Stoney's conversation.

"Joe, I need you to find Bucket and Julia and get them back out to the ranch."

"Done!"

Joe had last seen Bucket and Julia at the hospital emergency room and had seen to it that Bucket would at least have the burn on his hand looked at.

The couple had returned to the Cherry Farms house to get some rest. Bucket was drained physically and mentally. Julia was worried about him and persuaded him to close his eyes and get some sleep.

She made him some tea, sat with him on the sofa and then finally led him to the bed in Maggie's room.

Julia closed the door and curled up on the sofa in the living room and fell asleep.

Suddenly, she awoke and saw a flashing red light, pulsating through the living room window.

Startled, she jumped up and opened the screen door. It was Sheriff Arona.

"Joe what are you doing back out here?"

"It's Stoney, he wants you and Bucket to return to the ranch. It's important."

"Why? Bucket just fell asleep and I'd like to keep it that way. He's exhausted."

"Julia! Herman Smith is out at the ranch."

"Oh, no. I can't believe this!"

Joe had persuaded the couple to go with him in his police car. With lights flashing, Joe sped down I-17. Julia sat in the back seat and Bucket sat in the front passenger seat and stared out the window.

Bucket grumbled, "Why is he here? Why now? I'm not sure I can even look at the man."

Joe looked at the speedometer. He was hitting 85 miles an hour. They reached the Johnson gate in no time at all — at least twenty minutes sooner than it would have taken in Bucket's old pickup.

The squad car rolled over the cattle guard and five minutes later the ranch house was in sight.

A strange car was parked in front of the house. Bucket motioned to Julia. "The license plate on that car. It's the same number on the piece of paper in the jewelry box."

Julia looked at Bucket. "My, God!"

Stoney met the three of them at the front door.

"Thanks, Joe. You did good. I'll take it from here."

Stoney put his right arm on Bucket's shoulder. "Son, there's more you need to hear. Inside is the answers to all your questions. I think you should go in there alone. You need to do this. I know you're angry and have a right to be, but the man in there is lost, too, and needs to be found. I promise you, you'll walk out of here free of it all."

Bucket walked slowly into the den and sat down in the first chair he saw. He looked at the tall, gray-haired man and as Stoney had put it the man looked lost, tired and beaten.

"Herman Smith?"

The man turned. Tears ran down his cheek.

"Bucket?"

Herman moved forward to the edge of his seat and looked directly at Bucket.

"I've wrestled over and over in my head what to say to you, where to start and will I have the guts to let it all out. I must begin when I first met Maggie. It was at a dance hall in Prescott…"

Bucket adhered to Stoney's advice and sat there patiently with his eyes focused on the mouth of the man across from him.

Herman, who earlier had relived his past with Stoney, now needed to do it all over again — only this time he was facing a young man just six feet away from him and it wasn't just any man, it was his son.

Herman left no stone unturned. From his gambling addiction, to his inability to settle down and to his Las Vegas underworld connections. He let Bucket know of the hook the Malfonso Family had on him and Flame. He spoke of the gun battle in LA and the murderous rampage of the two men who ended the life of Flame Rafferty.

And the baby, yes the baby, and how they left LA and drove through Imperial Valley, on to Yuma and to Wickenburg. Then to a hardware store just outside of Prescott which sold oversized, steel buckets.

And finally to Cordes Junction and to the dirt road leading to Maggie's house.

"It had to be done. I knew you'd be safe in the hands of the most loving person I knew...Maggie Smith."

"Bucket, the baby was you and you ARE my son..."

Bucket, lowered his head and sobbed. "I don't think I can cry anymore."

Stoney sat on the porch with Julia, Alexandra, the girls and Sheriff Arona. He looked west toward the darkness. He heard the rider. He couldn't see him at first, but he heard the sound of the galloping Palomino, ridden by his foreman Dusty Rhoades.

The Palomino and its rider entered the compound and raced past the corral. Dusty was out of the saddle just a split second before he pulled in the reigns, bringing the horse to a halt.

"Stoney, there's three vehicles parked down the road. It looks like about six of them and they all have rifles in their hands."

Stoney noticed Bucket and Herman in the doorway, both with a concerned look on their faces. He looked at Herman and questioned him, "Are you sure this is over just money?"

"A lot of money. Close to a million," Herman said. "But there's more, one of the men at the apartment was one of the Malfonso brothers.

"My, God!" Stoney yelled.

Stoney looked around. There wasn't much time, but maybe just enough.

"Dusty get all the men together. Make sure they're armed. He threw a set of keys to his foreman. "There's enough rifles in the glass case in the main guesthouse, get 'em. Bucket...Herman, here's the keys to the basement. Through the first door by the kitchen, there is a couple of repeaters and a shotgun down there...and plenty of ammo."

"Damn, Stoney. Have you been expecting a war around here," yelled Bucket.

"No not really, most of them are collector's items...most of them have never been fired, but there's always a first time!"

"Herman you get all the women down to the basement and lock them in and get your butt back up here. Your Mafia-war ends tonight!"

"Joe, pull your squad car inside the barn and prepare yourself."

Stoney positioned his men.

Fully armed, Herman and Bucket headed for the barn and found their way to the loft. Stoney and Dusty headed for the roof. There was plenty of cover up there.

Stoney was angry. This was not his fight, but this was his ranch and he wasn't about to let some casino pinheads from Las Vegas come in and destroy what had taken him years to build.

It got deadly quiet.

Malfonso's men would come right down the dirt road. Stoney figured they weren't smart enough to come at them from another direction. There was one way in for them and one way out...in a coffin.

Bucket moved a couple bales of hay for additional cover. It wasn't a foxhole but close to it and soon they would come at them, only there wouldn't be as many as Joey Henderson and his platoon had to face just twelve months ago in Vietnam.

Herman sat back on a wooden slab near the window of the barn and put his newly acquired rifle on his shoulder and looked at his son. "I'm so sorry, Bucket. I know I have no right to call you, son, so I will just call you Bucket."

"Yeah, it is probably better if you did," said Bucket, who at the moment was more worried about staying alive.

"When I saw Maggie's obituary in the Prescott paper, I

think I knew what I had to do, but if it wasn't for Stoney I don't think I could have pulled it off."

"I was laid up at the Hotel Cordes overnight. The hotel clerk must have recognized me and called Stoney. I wanted to come clean, go to Maggie's gravesite and come clean with you. I needed help. I guess I've always needed help, but it had always been easier to run."

Bucket squirmed, repositioned his body and looked down the dirt road. Nothing. No car lights, no men with rifles in their hands...nothing but darkness.

"You've had it rough, Herman. I guess I wouldn't want to be in your shoes," Bucket said.

"Yes, it hasn't been easy for you, either. I was always on the run, but I'd pop into Prescott now and then, drive over and check up on you. I even saw three, maybe four of your basketball games. You were something else."

"You saw me play?"

"You bet I did. You played great and when you left for boot camp, I was there at Sky Harbor, too, hiding... watching you board your flight."

"I can't believe all this," said a shocked Bucket. "All these years, living a lie."

"Until now, Bucket. "Until now."

"When this is over and it'll be over soon, I promise you. Go to the basement and grab a hold of your gal. Hold her tight and build a life together. You've had enough misery for a lifetime, Bucket. Enough is enough."

Bucket looked at the man across from him and he just had to ask, "What was my mother like?"

"I don't think we have enough time for me to tell you about Flame. Yes, she was a card shark, tough as nails, hell-bent on following the same path I was on. She loved you, even though she held you in her arms for just two months. She lived a life with the hand that was dealt her. In many ways, she handled it better than I did. You have her eyes, her guts, but you have Maggie's upbringing and that's what really made you what you are today."

"And what is that?" Bucket questioned.

"A fine man, a leader. A human being who will go on and make something worthwhile out of your life.

I wish I had something to do with that. I had nothing to do with it, but I'm here now and I'll do my best to keep you alive. I can shoot you know. I've had plenty of time to practice."

"So can I. So can I," said Bucket, as he checked his ammo and took another look down the road."

"Then, I guess those guys out there are in trouble," said Herman, releasing his first smile in a long time.

Alexandra looked at a worried Julia and the two girls. "We're going to be all right. Stoney will get us out of this. When you hear five raps at the door, followed closely by another five, it'll be your Dad. It'll be Stoney. I promise you."

Julia wondered how Bucket was holding on. He had been through so much and now he must deal with a group of thugs from

Las Vegas, trying to shoot up a ranch and everybody in it.

She knew Bucket would save them. He was probably the most equipped to do so. A war hero who had plenty of shooting medals in his duffel bag to prove it. A duffel bag that was still unpacked, laying in the doorway at the Cherry Farms house. Oh, she thought, so much has happened in the past few days. It seemed like a lifetime had passed by her.

Stoney was first to see them. He motioned to Dusty. He took out his flashlight and signaled his men on the ridge and the three men in the barn.

The Malfonso gang left their cars behind. They were all dressed in black and they acted like they were out for a late-night stroll.

As they entered the compound, they scattered. The first shot came from the man on the right and the bullet sizzled by Bucket's right ear.

"Here they come!"

Fire rang out from the ridge north of the corral. The six men fled for cover. Stoney let loose from his spot on the roof and caught one man just above his left knee.

"I'm hit," the man yelled out.

"Stay down," another man said. "They've got men on the ridge... some in the barn and some on the roof of the main house. This isn't going to be a walk in the park!"

Bucket thought he saw movement on the south-side of the corral. He looked again and sure enough he found his target. He slowly pulled the trigger and waited. The bullet found its mark and exploded into the dark figure in the corral. The man grabbed at the fence post, but fell to the ground.

"Jesus!" another man yelled out. "They got Kelco. He's gone!"

Another round of fire rang out. A cowhand on the ridge was hit. The five men left fired at will toward the roof of the ranch house. Stoney fired back, but took a bullet in the shoulder. Dusty grabbed him and both men crawled to the north-side of the roof.

"A cowhand has been hit and I think Stoney has taken some lead in his shoulder," Bucket shouted.

Two men charged the ranch house, but Herman fired three shots and the last bullet caught the man in his right thigh. The other man tried to reach the porch, but Bucket dropped him with one shot as he fell back and bounced off Stoney's Jeep, falling face down to the ground.

Another man had reached the entrance to the barn and tried to unlock the latch. He was greeted with Joe's squad car. The vehicle, with the red light blazing, barreled through the barn door and took out the intruder.

"Sorry about that," Joe said, as he turned the man over and felt his pulse. "He's done."

"There's just two left," Bucket yelled out as he glanced over to Herman. Herman was gone.

Herman jumped over the squad car, passed by Joe, and headed for the corral, yelling at the top of his lungs, "Come and get me!"

Bucket realized his father was calling them out. He grabbed onto the rope, slid down and hit the ground running.

The two Mafia men fired in unison and unleashed a ray of bullets into the chest of Herman Smith. Herman went to his knees. He looked back, searching for one last look at Bucket. His rifle slipped from his grasp and he fell to the ground.

Stoney fired from the roof top and took out the man on the right. Bucket kept walking straight for the last black-suited man standing and fired six shots into his chest. The man pulled the trigger four more times, but every shot went skyward. The man staggered, took two more steps and landed on top of Herman's body.

Bucket rushed to Herman's side and grabbed the man. He was still breathing. Bucket looked into the eyes of the Mafia hit man, who was searching desperately for his final breath…his dying words, "I got my man."

Bucket held the man close, looked into his eyes one more time, shook him and then pushed him back to the ground.

Bucket reached for his father. Herman held out his hand and

looked into his son's eyes. "Enough is enough, Bucket... it is time to go."

"You can call me son, Herman. You can call me, son!"

Herman smiled and closed his eyes.

Bucket held his father close as two helicopters hovered overhead.

A row of police cars with lights flashing rambled over the cattle guard, sped down the road and entered the compound. The officers brought the vehicles to a screeching stop, got out of their cars and with guns drawn eyed the scene in front of them. The gun battle was over. It looked like something you would see in the final frame of a Western movie. Only this was Stoney Johnson's ranch, not a movie set.

Alexandra, Julia and the girls listened. First it was five knocks and then five more. They opened the door and the Johnson girls fell into the arms of a wounded Stoney, his left shoulder covered in blood.

Julia rushed up the stairs and out the front door and into the arms of Bucket.

"It's over, Julia. "It's over."

Bucket looked up at the sky. He then looked north toward the town of Cordes Junction. In his mind he could see clearly the cemetery at the top of the hill which overlooked the normal, peaceful town he grew up in.

He remembered the beautiful flowers he had placed in front of Maggie's gravesite, just days ago.

Bucket lifted his right hand toward the sky, "Rest in peace, Maggie. Rest in peace."

# Chapter 6

## The Malfonso Way

Cordes Junction Sheriff Bucket Smith tossed the front page of the Phoenix Gazette into the trash can.

The gun battle at Stoney Johnson's ranch not only made the daily papers in the state of Arizona, but made national news. The word had spread making Bucket an instant hero.

The reporters from newspapers and magazines across

the state were relentless. It had been three months and Bucket was still fielding calls. "Sheriff, could I set up an interview? Could I send a photographer and takes some photos of you in uniform?"

Bucket sat at his desk. It was early Monday morning. He had a lot of paper work to complete, but he wasn't in the mood to tackle it. Instead, he poured himself another cup of coffee, sat back and eyed the two photos on his desk — one of Maggie Smith and the other of his wife, Julia.

So much had happened. Even as strong as he was — a seasoned

war veteran who had seen so much death at home and abroad — it was hard for him to handle at times, hard for him to let it all go and build a life with Julia. He picked up Julia's photo, smiled and returned the picture to the right corner of his desk.

Julia and Bucket were newlyweds. They were married just 28 days ago. They said their vows at the First Methodist Church in downtown Cordes Junction and spent their honeymoon on Coronado Island in San Diego.

The wedding was the talk of the county. It was literally standing room only at the small white Victorian-style church on the corner of First Street and Elm. The Rev. Elmer Thompson had overseen more than 200 weddings in his 20 years of service to the community, but the Bucket Smith — Julia Childress wedding was one he'd never forget. Inquisitive onlookers from around the state motored through the streets of Cordes, hoping to get a glimpse of the newlyweds on their wedding day.

Of course, the wedding reception was held at the Johnson

ranch as Stoney and his wife, Alexandra, opened the gate, allowing the townsfolk in to enjoy the festivities — including pig roasting ceremonies and a barn dance, followed with an array of fireworks to complete the occasion.

The Phoenix Gazette ran a full-page spread in its bridal section and photos of the wedding surfaced as far away as San Diego, Los Angeles and Las Vegas. The reporters and photographers followed the young couple all the way to the beaches along Coronado Island.

Bucket picked up Maggie's picture, shook his head and carefully placed the photo to its rightful place on his desk.

He pushed his chair back, stood up and walked across his office to the window. He looked down on Main Street and then looked north toward the Cordes Junction Cemetery. The cemetery was barely visible from the window, but the image in his head of Maggie's final resting place was front and center in his thoughts.

"Maggie, oh Maggie...rest in peace."

The powers-to-be in the town of Cordes Junction had been good to him. When Sheriff Joe Arona resigned his position shortly after the gun battle, it was inevitable that Bucket Smith, the local hero, would be offered the job.

Arona had certainly put in his years of service — thirty to be exact, and he felt it was time to grab his pension, sell his house and move to Green Valley, a retirement community south of Tucson. "I think I'll hang up my spurs and play some golf."

It took some prodding by Mayor Roman Walker, Judge Samuel Criner and the town's top citizen, Stoney Johnson, to get Bucket to accept the job. They took it slow and allowed Bucket time to think it over. Bucket gave it a lot of thought, but in the end he accepted the job, after all he would soon have a wife to support...and they planned to have a baby in the near future.

Bucket moved away from the window and noticed the picture on the north wall of his office was crooked. On the way back to his desk he stopped to adjust the black and white photo of Stoney,

Maggie and a little boy, all sitting on the steps of the Johnson ranch house. Bucket figured he must have been about nine years old at the time. He quickly remembered those happy times he spent on the ranch — fishing, hunting and hanging around with the cowhands in the bunkhouse.

The little boy in the photo had no idea the twist and turns he would face as he grew into a man. Ironically, the Johnson ranch, which at one time was his playground, would turn into a battlefield and turn his life upside down at the age of twenty-five.

The phone on Bucket's desk rang out.

Bucket answered the call on the third ring. "It's me, honey," Julia said. "Are you going to be on time tonight? I'm cooking your favorite, pork chops."

"That's great!" Bucket said. "I need to stop by Stoney's hardware store and pick up a few things, but I should be home by six o'clock."

"You be sure to say hello to Mary."

Mary Hamilton was the new manager at the hardware store.

She had taken over the position, replacing Julia, who had ran the business for Stoney for so many years. Julia needed to concentrate on one thing: her husband.

That alone will be a full-time job.

Santiago Malfonso maneuvered his four-year-old Cadillac off Highway 89 and turned left and headed to downtown Prescott. He was looking for the Hassayampa Inn, a landmark hotel which had been built back in the 1920s. He had read good reviews about the place and supposedly he had a room reserved on the top floor of the establishment, overlooking the famous downtown area and the famous drinking holes along a street called Whiskey Row.

Santiago was the oldest of the Malfonso sons and he was certainly no spring chicken. In fact, he was close to retirement age, not that he was expecting a retirement check anytime soon, like never — hit men like him rarely file taxes.

His father, Sam Malfonso, was on his deathbed, tucked away in his bedroom at the family home south of Las Vegas, complete with nurses to tend to his every need. The old man still ran the underground business, even at the age of 92. Sam was a vengeful man and he had one dying wish: revenge the death of three of his sons.

Gambler Herman Smith was responsible for the death of Rocco Malfonso more than 25 years ago in a shootout near Los Angeles and more recently in a gun battle at some wild horse ranch in Arizona, two more brothers were lost, Anthony and Sammy. The two brothers had completed their mission all right, They finally got their man. Sammy was credited with the kill as he poured six shots into the chest of Herman Smith.

Santiago knew it was Bucket Smith who had returned fire on that day at the ranch. He had a stack of clippings in his briefcase to prove it. He remembers his father slamming a lamp against a wall and trashing his desk when he had heard the news of this Bucket Smith ending the life of his youngest boy. His father's face turned bright red. He had seen the anger in his father before, but nothing could come close to the way his father acted upon hearing the news.

It was the final straw. All the life in his father's body seemed to float out of the room. The old man slumped in his chair "This Herman Smith takes down my Rocco and now it's the son...this Bucket Smith, who takes the last breath from Anthony and my young boy... my precious Sammy!"

Santiago figured this would be his final job. His final killings. It was time to get out of the business, find this Bucket Smith and some John Wayne wannabe, a rancher called Stoney Johnson.

Take them down. Then leave the country and settle somewhere in Costa Rica — far from Las Vegas and far from the family business.

Santiago just weeks ago had sat down next to his father's bed and listened to the dying man's order, "get Bucket Smith... whatever it takes, get him."

Yes, Santiago and his father had seen all the photos and all the headlines about the two men who took down Anthony and Sammy. They had seen the wedding pictures of the perfect couple, Bucket and Julia Smith. They had seen plenty of pictures of some Arizona rancher who helped Bucket Smith make a laughing stock out of the Malfonso Family. They were all smiling and upright, while Tony and Sammy were gone, buried six-feet under.

Bucket raced up the steps and into the arms of Julia. He held her tight and kissed her.

"It's good to be home," Bucket said. "I can smell those pork chops."

"Hold on now. Sit yourself down. I'll get you a glass of wine.

You sit back in the lazy chair and relax."

Bucket sat back and eyed the living room.

"I can't believe what you've done to the place in a few short weeks."

"It's our home — your home. I love you, Bucket."

Bucket glanced at the television. Julie had the sound turned down. The news was on and it was a special report from Las Vegas. Bucket grabbed a hold of the remote and turned the sound up.

"Julia, listen to this!"

"Crime boss Sam Malfonso died today at his home in Boulder City, Nevada — a town just 40 miles south of Las Vegas, just weeks before his trial for tax evasion, extortion and his responsibility regarding a gun battle which took place in Arizona three months ago. Seven people died that day — including two Malfonso brothers, Anthony and Sam. Jr.," stated the reporter Mary Anne Mobley.

The reporter continued, "Also, authorities have not been able to locate Sam Malfonso's oldest son, Santiago, the remaining member of the Malfonso family. The funeral for the crime boss is scheduled for next Sunday and the proceedings will be under tight security."

"This never ends," shouted Bucket, as he stood up and put his arm around Julia.

"What does this mean, Bucket?"

"It means the Malfonso family is through and once they catch up with Santiago, they can close the books on one of the most notorious underground crime syndicates in Las Vegas. He's probably already out of the country. Chances are he's got plenty of money in a foreign bank somewhere."

"I don't understand this world sometimes," Julia said. "Why do these thugs exists and how do they get away with all this?"

"It's all about money and power," Bucket said. "These people want it all and they don't care how they get it."

Bucket took Julia's hand, "Let's get out of here and go for a walk."

Bucket was back in his office the following morning. It had been a busy couple of hours. There had been a break-in at the auto parts store. At first glance it looked to be a job done by a couple of teenagers, missing were a couple of socket sets and a case of 30-weight oil.

The big case of the day: the rescue of Betty Hudson's cat, Tilly. Tilly, one of six cats owned by the widowed Hudson, had scampered up a giant oak tree and couldn't get down. One call to the Cordes Fire Department, took care of the episode.

Deputy Wanda Ridgeway entered Bucket's office.

Wanda was a jack-of-all-trades around the office, she'd answer the phone, file papers and make coffee. Wanda was the mother of three and only worked twenty hours a week, but was always on call in case Bucket needed her to handle a situation — a situation which wouldn't require a revolver.

Wanda loved her job and was content with keeping the office in spotless condition. She left the hard field work to the Simpson twin brothers, Matt and Mark — a couple of hunks. It was tough, at first glance, distinguishing the difference between the two. Matt had a slight scar on his forehead and she practically had to kiss him to discover which brother she was talking to.

"Bucket, there is someone here to see you."

In walked Freddie Greathouse.

"You've got to be kidding me," Bucket exclaimed. "I haven't seen you since 1958. What the heck are you doing back in town?"

"I'm with the FBI, working out of the Phoenix division. They sent me up here to see you and I jumped at the chance to get up here and see my old basketball buddy."

"I do remember reading about a Freddie Greathouse with the FBI in Phoenix...some journal I was reading...or it might have been a newspaper article. I didn't think it was the same Greathouse who outscored me my senior year in high school."

"This is I old buddy. Speaking of news articles, boy have you been in the news."

"Don't remind me," Bucket said, offering his high school buddy a chair.

"Well, Bucket. We have something in common other than basketball."

"What is that, may I ask?"

"The Malfonso brothers. I was assigned to their case the first year

I was with the bureau. Back when I first got started in this business, back in New Jersey. Man, they have a long list of criminal activity, except drugs and I can't believe they stayed away from that hot potato."

Bucket listened attentively as Freddie summed up the Malfonso file.

"So, there you have it. I asked the higher ups to give me a shot at coming up here. Heck, I was born here and I heard about the run-in my good buddy had with some of the Malfonso brothers."

"Run-in...it was more like an all out war."

"Yeah, I know. I'm up to date and I just might be a little ahead of the curve, which is another reason I'm sitting across from you at this very moment."

"What do you mean by that?" asked Bucket.

"Well, the rumor is Santiago Malfonso is long gone...maybe he's already deep in Mexico by now, but I don't think so. I think he's coming here and his M.O. has always been revenge, just like his old man."

"My, God, I said to Julia last night that this thing was never going to be over. My intuition was telling me so. I've had that sixth sense...that ache in the back of my neck...telling me to keep my eyes open."

"Well, you're right about that, Bucket. I'm going to stay a while, over at the Hotel Cordes and I'm going to cling to you like a wet blanket. He's coming. I'm sure of it. Chances are he'll bring some thugs with him...hire them at top dollar. Heck, he's out of brothers, his father is gone and all the

Malfonso holdings have been seized by the IRS, as of today."

"This isn't good. I need to ride out to the Johnson ranch. Stoney and his family need to be warned. It might be a good idea to get his family out of town for a while. Now, Stoney...he's a different story. He'll want to protect that ranch of his. He's gonna offer his help and knowing Stoney...he won't take no for an answer."

Freddie added that five men out of the FBI office in Phoenix are assigned to the case and are focusing on a 200-mile radius from Phoenix north to Camp

Verde and the area from Prescott to Black Canyon City.

"The higher ups are only going so far with me on this. That's why we have just a few agents available. They still believe he's heading for Mexico."

The two men looked at each other. They both knew the answer. Santiago Malfonso was coming.

"One thing I forgot to tell you, Bucket."

"What's that?"

"Santiago Malfonso is a crack shot and he can handle explosives."

# Chapter 7

The clerk at the Hassayampa Inn handed the room key to the dark-tanned, gray-haired gentleman and pointed him in the direction of the elevator. "Number 43, fourth floor, third room on the right...great room...overlooks Gurley Street."

"Much obliged," said the man.

Santiago unlocked the door. The room was what he had expected. He had a good view of the street below. He could see people scurrying up and down the sidewalk. They all looked like they were in a hurry to get to their legal jobs and put in the their usual forty hours a week and take home a couple of measly checks a month — just enough to pay their bills.

Of course, Santiago couldn't begin to understand what it was like to make an honest living. He had survived more than sixty of his adult years on the wrong side of the law. He followed in his father's footsteps. None of the Malfonso sons got away from the business. Not one of them broke away from their father's hold on them.

Santiago closed the curtain. Suddenly, he felt very alone. He would have to get used to it.

"I'm the only one left," Santiago said, under his breath.

He took his gun out of his holster and placed it on the night stand. He shuffled off his Florsheim shoes, puffed up a pillow and stretched out on the bed. He said those words again, "I'm the only one left."

There was no brother to call, no father to speak to. Santiago had talked to his father ten days ago and the man could barely speak then and besides chances are the family home was probably bugged. As for his mother? Well, she passed away eight years ago. She just got tired of it all. She died a wrinkled old woman at the age of 72.

Santiago took a deep breath and looked around his room. He had one last job ahead of him and then he'd disappear and for the first time in his life he would be free. He'd change his name, buy a boat and he would spend what was left of his golden years away from it all.

Santiago shook his head. How does a hit man enjoy life? He knew he had paid the price for more than a half a century. As a little boy in New Jersey, he'd tag along with his father — in and out of every speakeasy joint in town. His father was a loan shark then and if the customers didn't pay up, chances are their body would be found in the East River.

Sam Malfonso was the worst of them. Santiago had no chance... no chance at all for a normal life. Instead, he followed in his father's footsteps and became a carbon copy of the ruthless crime boss.

He was branded a Malfonso from the beginning and now, as he eyed the ceiling fan above him, Santiago figured he was at the end of the road. He was tired. He had resigned himself to the fact, he'd either go out in a blaze of glory, or if he was lucky — and he'd always been lucky, he'd survive and disappear...never to be heard from again.

He thought back to his childhood days, playing hide and seek with his brothers. Things were so simply then. Sammy could never hide from him very long. Sammy was always the first one to be tagged, while Rocco and Anthony were a bit more cagey— always the last to be caught.

Why did he have to grow up? Why was it written in stone that the offspring of Sam Malfonso would be destined to become killers...destined for a life of crime, members of an underground crime syndicate — surfacing only when there was a job to do...an order to carry out...an execution to complete.

Each killing took more and more out of him. Santiago wanted out. He had his fill of it all, but he couldn't let his guard down. He needed to set his final plan into place. He needed to complete his last mission and then it would all be over...for good.

His plan was simple.

Santiago saw to it his hired guns would have an out-of-the-way place to hold up. They'd be arriving in less than forty-eight hours. There were six of them — none of them had made it through the sixth grade. They were born killers, not much different front him, but they were a crazy bunch and they thought of only one thing: the $25,000 payout they would each receive upon completion of their assignment.

The ranch was hidden deep in the hills behind the quiet little town of Mayer. Santiago's first mistake was giving each of the men $5,000 of upfront money. He hoped they hadn't gambled it all away in Laughlin, or spent it all on whiskey and wild women. He expected them to show up on time or there would be hell to pay.

The ranch was just five miles directly west of Cordes Junction.

Santiago was tired of talking to himself. He put his shoes on, put his revolver back in his holster, grabbed his hat and coat and headed out the door. He looked like any other old-timer in town — except for the piece he had hidden just under his left shoulder.

He entered the lobby and tipped his hat to the clerk.

The clerk responded, "Have a nice dinner, Mr. Jorgensen." Earlier in the day, Santiago remembered to change out the plates on his car. He had signed the guest register at the hotel as Lloyd Jorgensen from Minnesota — even went as far as writing the plate number down for the unsuspecting clerk.

The sun was setting as he left the hotel lobby. He walked west along the sidewalk — heading for Whiskey Row and a couple of rum and cokes at the Birdcage

Saloon. It took him less than five minutes to get to the entrance of the Birdcage. The watering hole was crowded, just as well he thought. He did manage to find a stool at the bar, settled in and mingled with the crowd.

He felt right at home in a tavern. Heck, most people didn't even bother to ask his name or where he was from...most of them were wallowing in their own misery. There were a couple of pool games in progress in the back room, but even though he was good at the game, getting in a pool game would bring too much attention his way...and he didn't need that.

He had a job to do. His job was a lot different than the rest of clientele at the bar. He was sure of it. In a few days, he would destroy a town and take out its hero — the sheriff.

Santiago ordered a second drink and eyed his hands. They were steady, He had nerves of steel when it came to killing people. He was calm under fire. His father had helped him with that. His father would always say, "Chances are you're unlikely to face someone who has been through what you have. Remember, you're gonna have the upper hand. Play it smart, analyze the situation and then get the job done."

He looked around. For a moment, he thought he heard his father's voice as a man passed by with his arm around a woman. The man was built like his father and even shuffled as he walked, much like his father did. Santiago turned back to the bar. There were those words again, "I'm the only one left."

Santiago glanced at the television above the bar. It was a

good thing he did. He jumped off his stool and moved to his left a couple of feet. He caught the tail end of the TV anchor's report.

"Crime boss Sam Malfonso died today at his family home in Boulder City, Nevada. Malfonso, 92, was scheduled to go on trial for tax evasion, extortion and murder in just two weeks. Funeral arrangements are set for Sunday morning at the Desert Lawn Cemetery in Las Vegas. The authorities are on the lookout for the oldest and the only remaining son of the crime boss, Santiago Malfonso. The funeral will be under tight security...in other news..."

Santiago slid a ten dollar bill under his glass and left the Birdcage, slowly...careful not to draw any attention to himself. His eyes glassy. He headed up Gurley Street, alone in his thoughts. Under his breath, he uttered the same words again, "I'm the only one left."

Freddie and Bucket were on the road quickly. They sped up I-17 in Freddie's white Ford Fairlane. Bucket looked west toward the mountains. It was another clear day with blue sky as far as the eye could see.

Bucket motioned to Freddie that the entrance to Stoney's ranch was just ahead. "You'll have to use the phone just to the right of the gate, a new addition to the place since the shootout."

Freddie got out of his car, picked up the phone and within seconds the gate opened. "The ranch house is about a mile in — just a mile from where it all went down."

"You have been deep in thought, haven't you good buddy?"

"Yes, I have. Yes, I have."

Stoney greeted the new arrivals and shuffled them into his den.

Bucket had sat in Stoney's den just three months ago and listened to Stoney's tale of Maggie and Herman Smith — listened, and then squirmed in his seat, as Stoney, reluctantly, unleashed all of Maggie and Herman's secrets, while shattering Bucket's past and all his childhood memories in the process.

That day will forever be lodged in his mind. How he survived that day and the months that followed was due to the love and support from Julia...from Stoney, his godfather — a fact Bucket discovered during all the turmoil. The day which ended in a gun battle and the death of seven people — including the life of his father, a man he knew for less than twenty-four hours.

"Stoney you're looking a lot better. How's the shoulder?"

Bucket said, as the rancher handed the two men a beer.

"I can't believe it. It's as good as new. Went out to the gun range yesterday. My 30-30 was smoldering...didn't miss a target."

Bucket shook his head and turned to Freddie.

"This guy can hit anything from two-hundred yards out...just look at that rack," Bucket said, as he pointed to the north end of the den and the huge elk head on the wall.

Freddie smiled and then got right to the point. "Mr. Johnson."

"Call me, Stoney."

"Stoney, I'm Fred Greathouse, special agent with the FBI and I'm assigned to the Malfonso case and we have reason to believe Santiago Malfonso is heading this way."

"Haven't we seen enough of those guys?"

"There's a good possibility he may be after you and Bucket, payback for killing his brothers."

Greathouse went on to explain to Stoney his reasoning on why he assumes Malfonso is heading for the ranch. "To him this is the scene of the crime. He lost two brothers here and to make matters worse his father died yesterday at the Malfonso Estate."

Greathouse summarized his feelings on the matter and ended by saying, "Chances are good he'll be bringing an army this time."

Stoney sat down in his leather chair behind his desk. "I need to get my family out of here. You'd think that thug would try to get himself out of the country, but there's no understanding these people...the first time they came here...they just walked right up and started blasting away."

Bucket stood up and walked over to the fireplace and eyed the picture on the mantel — a picture of Maggie, Bucket, Stoney and his family.

"We've got to prepare, Stoney." Bucket said. "My office is small, but I have my deputies already canvassing the roads in and out of here and up and down I-17 from Cordes to Camp Verde. Freddie has five agents in the area and the FBI office in Phoenix is on alert. We'll get them...we've done it before, we'll do it again."

Santiago was up early the next morning. He ate breakfast at a cafe near the hotel and then walked the four blocks to the rent-a-car company. "I'm interested in a jeep, need it for a week."

"Sure thing," said the young man with wavy blond hair and dressed in a tank top and a pair of plaid Bermuda shorts. "It's been a crazy day. Three men from Wisconsin showed up first thing this morning and rented the last three vans I had on the lot and now you show up out of the blue and want a Jeep. I think I've got one left."

"Business must be good. Any chance you can get this completed. I've got somewhere I need to be."

"Sure thing, Mr. Jorgensen," said the sales agent as he eyed the credit card. "Let me fill out the paperwork, run the card through and I'll be right back with the keys."

Santiago returned to the hotel parking lot and pulled into the space next to his Cadillac. He had made one last stop at the closest hardware store. He picked up a couple pair of wire cutters, two coolers, seven sets of gloves and a light brown golf hat.

The fifty-something cashier had asked. "You in town for some golf?"

"No, never played the game, just like the hat."

Santiago shook his head. The cashier was oblivious to the fact he had just bought seven sets of gloves and some wire cutters, but the golf hat got her attention.

"You, play?"

"No way, but my husband certainly does. Only thing is...the man spends more time at the bar, afterwards. He calls it the 19th hole."

Santiago tipped the brim of his newly acquired hat and left the hardware store.

It was mid-morning and the parking lot was empty.

He looked around and quickly opened the trunk of his car. The trunk was practically full. Two golf bags took up most of the room. He pulled out a briefcase and crammed the coolers in the trunk, along with the sack of goodies he had just bought at the hardware store.

He closed the truck and headed for the back entrance to the hotel.

Bucket and Freddie left Stoney's ranch convinced that his wife Alexandra and his daughters, Katherine Anne and Judy, would visit relatives for a couple of weeks.

Alexandra would take the girls to Flagstaff and stay with Stoney

Jr., her stepson and Stoney's oldest son. Stoney's son recently graduated from Northern Arizona University and landed an upper management job with the United States Forest Service.

As for Stoney, he wasn't going anywhere. His first order of business was to gather ammo and check on his arsenal in the basement of the main house. He would need to clue in the cowhands and prepare them for another fight...another battle with a bunch of thugs from Las Vegas.

Freddie made it back to Cordes in record time, dropped

Bucket off at his office and headed back to the hotel. He needed to make some calls — including checking in with his office in Phoenix.

Bucket checked in with his deputies, the Simpson twins. Everything was quiet...no strangers in town...nothing out of the ordinary...another quiet day and night in Cordes Junction.

Bucket cleaned up his desk and called Wanda.

"Everything is fine at the office. The phone hardly rang most of the day, but I've got my radio with me. Call me if you need anything. Got spaghetti cooking, need to feed some hungry kids."

"That's great, Wanda. I'm heading home."

Julia sat on the front porch, awaiting Bucket's arrival. She sipped on a glass of tea. An hour ago she planted another rose bush on the west side of the house — she now had four of them planted, all in a neat and perfectly placed row.

She picked up her planting and gardening skills from Mildred

Dunworthy — Maggie's best friend and partner in crime. The same woman who had helped raise Bucket during his childhood years... the same woman that Maggie confided in on the day Bucket was left on the front porch...the very same porch Julia was now sitting in — sipping on what was left of her ice tea.

Julia shook her head as she recalled what lengths Maggie and Mildred had gone to in order to keep the family secret from the townspeople.

The two woman concocted a story about why the little fella

suddenly appeared. As the story goes, Maggie's Aunt Belle, from back east, had passed away in a car accident, along with her husband. The baby survived the crash, pulled from the wreckage, crying, but alive and well...and all alone.

The story seemed to work.

Things were now coming together, Julia thought, as she eyed the dirt road, waiting patiently for Bucket and that cruiser of his to make another appearance on Cherry Farms Road. Their time together was precious...the two of them had been through so much in such a short time.

Julia placed her glass of tea on the table next to the hand-woven straw chair. The rocker swung back and forth as she stepped off the porch and headed for the big oak tree, just fifty steps from the main house. She sat in the swing — the old swing Bucket had played on many, many times during his childhood.

She glanced back at the house. Such a lovely home, she thought. A circular driveway led up to the house. Hedges surrounded the front of the old farm house. One large picture window in the living room allowed for a perfect view of the tall oak tree, the driveway and Cherry Farms Road. Small windows were situated on both sides of the house with green colored awnings attached to each one of them, cutting down the direct sunlight in the early morning hours, while filtering in just enough of the sun during the evening hours — still allowing for great views of the beautiful Arizona sunsets.

As for the barn, north of the house — still a work in progress, but Bucket did manage to clean out the loft — the loft he used to hide in as a young boy. In the breezeway was the old pickup truck, which hadn't moved a bit. In fact, the battery had gone dead and two of the tires were flat. Bucket had a lot of work to do on the truck, before he could cruise down Main Street on a Sunday afternoon, looking for a cold root beer at the A&W.

Julia jumped off the swing and marked her progress, just like Bucket used to do. "Okay," she said, "that's one foot further. Good job," clapping her hands, as if she had just set the world record in swing jumping.

She wandered over to the wooded fence that separated the house and the east pasture. She remembers how distraught Bucket was when he had raced home on the day he found out the family secret. He took his anger out on the piece of ground which once housed his makeshift basketball court — his favorite childhood spot.

Bucket set fire to his court...his playground. Julie cringed and muttered to herself, How did Bucket survive it all?

He survived all right as Julie turned and looked up the dusty road. Bucket was on his way.

Bucket parked his cruiser, gave Julia a hug and a kiss and then looked at her with a concerned luck. "I've got some bad news."

"What's wrong, Bucket?"

"You remember Freddie Greathouse?"

"Of course I do. He's that little guard who outscored you in high school. I heard he got a job with the FBI, but I lost track of him, heard he was working in New Jersey."

"Just to set the record straight he outscored me my senior year, but I had the edge in career points."

"Oh, honey, really," Julia said with a slight grin on her face. "Why do you bring his name up?"

"He's in town. He's working out of the Phoenix office and he's assigned to the Malfonso case."

Bucket went on to fill his wife in on just how much Freddie knew about the Malfonso brothers and the more she listened to the story, the more nervous Julia got.

"Oh, Bucket. This is awful. What are we going to do?"

"We're going to take care of this Santiago Malfonso. Don't you worry. There's FBI men all over this area and my deputies are patrolling the entrances and exits to town. Until this is over, I want you to stay put...stay safe. They may go after Stoney's ranch again."

"Oh, no!"

"Alexandra and the girls are going to stay in Flagstaff for a few weeks and Stoney, well you know Stoney, he's preparing his cowboys for another showdown."

Matt Simpson checked the time.

He was in the last hour of his shift. It was a boring day — one poor soul had a flat tire two miles north of the Cordes Junction turnoff, luckily the man had a spare and the deputy kept the traffic moving while the man, cursing under his breath, struggled with the tire iron but eventually got the job done and was ready to return to the road. "I'm going to miss my daughter's play over in Cottonwood...I'll make it up to her somehow."

"Take it easy," said the deputy, "no reason to add a speeding ticket to your evening. Good evening, Mr. Jones."

Deputy Simpson returned to Cordes and made his final run down Main Street, drove by the Valley National Bank, the library, the high school and made a right turn on to Second Street, all the businesses were closed up tighter than a drum — including Stoney Johnson's hardware store.

The parking lot at the Hotel Cordes, over on Johnson Street, was only half full, Deputy Simpson wasn't surprised. After all, it was Thursday, seven o'clock in the evening, and everyone was laying low until the weekend. Matt maneuvered his cruiser into his assigned space. Like he figured, his brother, Mark, was already in the office.

Mark was a night owl. He loved the night shift and it wasn't unusual for him to show up an hour before his scheduled time.

Bucket was lucky to have the Simpson brothers as his deputies. They were both young and aggressive, eager to learn and eager to succeed in their chosen profession. Their father retired with the highway patrol back in 1946 and their grandfather was a homicide detective for the City of Tucson back in the 40s. Both the father and the grandfather attended Matt and Mark's graduation in 1964 when the boys received their degrees in Criminal Justice from Arizona State University.

Bucket said to Julia recently, "Those Simpson brothers are so young."

Julia smiled and said to Bucket. "Honey, they're just three years younger than you."

Deep down Julia knew exactly what Bucket meant. Bucket had seen it all in his 25 years. Unfortunately, Bucket grew up fast...too fast.

## Chapter 8

Johnny Sylvester took out a pack of Camel cigarettes from his shirt pocket, cut open the top of the pack, banged the packet on his desk and continued to light up. He threw the rest of the pack on his desk and muttered to himself, "God awful habit."

He was 68 years old and smoking was one of those habits he couldn't break, the other was the whiskey...loved the Jim Beam about as much as the camels.

It was the end of the day, Sylvester owned a crop dusting business on the outskirts of Phoenix. A former airline pilot,

Sylvester owned enough land east of Goodyear to have a runway big enough to accommodate a couple of his overworked Cessna's and big enough to land and takeoff his big baby, a nine-passenger, Beechcraft Queen Air.

When talking about the old Beechcraft, he'd tell anyone who'd listen, "The darn thing goes through a lot of oil, but on a clear day I can gas her up and make it all the way to San Diego."

Sylvester was ready to close up shop when two men entered his office. The crop duster knew he was in trouble. "What can I do for you fellas?"

"Plenty!"

The isolated ranch in the hills behind the small town of Mayer wasn't much to look at. Santiago had paid some old woman $2,000 dollars...no questions asked. He felt good about the woman. She lived up in Sedona and Santiago had a connection, who had a connection and put him in touch with her.

With the money safe in her hand, she advised Santiago how to get to the ranch and how he could find the keys to the place, hidden in a box, in a hole, at the base of the big Saguaro — just to the left of the corral. "I'll have the electricity turned on by the time you get there."

As for his six cronies, they hated it.

Razor Head Jackson was the most vocal about it. "Is this the best you can do?"

"Deal with it, Jackson," said a very annoyed Santiago. "Three of you can sleep in the bunkhouse out back and there is three bedrooms and a den in here. We'll hit the road early Saturday and if we're lucky this business will all be behind us by high noon."

"I'm all for that," said Judd Snyder, the youngest man of the six. "I'll check out the bunkhouse."

"Good. There's a couple of coolers in the jeep full of beer. Why don't the rest of you figure out where you want to bed down. We'll have a few beers, get some shut-eye and in the morning we'll go over the plan one more time."

Santiago grabbed his briefcase and set up shop in the den. He opened the briefcase and spread a handful of maps on the table. He took a deep breath, sat down and dreamed of Costa Rica.

He figured Razor Head would be the toughest one to deal with and the young one, Judd, wouldn't be a problem. As for the other four — Jimmy McBride, Chester Owens, Kip Wells and Billy Bob Sorenson, he hadn't quite got a handle on them yet.

He figured they'd get the job done. The poor souls knew if they followed through and completed the job, the money would be waiting for them. They each had a key to a locker at a train station in San Diego — their money safely tucked way inside the locker, wrapped in paper bags — their reward for their part in the attack on Cordes Junction.

The day had gone as planned, Santiago had found his way to the ranch. He had the rear of the Jeep loaded with two large golf bags. When Santiago hit the highway, he figured no one would give him a second look. He looked like some old-timer on his way to a golf outing. Little did they know what was hidden beneath the sawed-off clubs.

Surprisingly, the six men showed up on time. The three vans were already hidden in the barn — all loaded and ready for action.

Two hours later, all the beer was gone and everyone was asleep — except Santiago. He stared out the window and into the night sky. There were those words again, "I'm the only one left."

The next day was uneventful for Bucket and Stoney Johnson. Quiet, too quiet. Stoney had sent Alexandra and the girls on their way. They should be halfway to Flagstaff by now, he thought. His cowhands were in place — some on horseback, watching over the area along I-17 and the entrance to the ranch, while others were hidden from sight, inside the compound.

Bucket was spending his Friday evening at home with Julia. It was quiet around Cherry Farms, except for the sounds, three miles away — just outside the eastern end of his property, where he could here the dragsters revving up their engines.

The teenagers needed somewhere to go on a Friday night. It was noisy for a couple of hours and then the kids would pack up and head back to town. The old drag strip was about three-quarters of a mile long, built by Cory Wilkerson in the early 1950s. Wilkerson owned the local auto parts store and had visions of making the property into a Speedway — complete with enough bleachers to accommodate all the racing fans of Cordes Junction.

Wilkerson got the strip completed, but passed away a month later of a heart attack. His son, Cody, took over the auto parts store, but apart from ramrodding the Friday Night Run

— as he called it, there were no plans to continue his father's dream. Times were tough and Cody could barely keep his business afloat.

"The dragsters are quiet tonight. Must not be a lot of races," Bucket said.

Julia didn't mind the noise, it was too quiet...too calm for her.

Bucket and Julia were more concerned about what was going on to the west of them...west of Cherry Farms Road. "Have you seen Freddie today?"

"Saw him early this morning, but he's out there with his men. We're well covered."

Bucket turned up his radio to clear the static on his emergency channel. "This all may be a false alarm, maybe Freddie has it all wrong and Malfonso is gone...out of the country for good. He certainly has enough backing in the crime world to make that happen."

"I wish he was gone for good!"

"So do I," Bucket said, knowing his confrontation with

Santiago Malfonso was inevitable. "I'm going to leave you this old radio. It's going to be a hectic weekend and if you see or hear anything unusual, you call me right away."

"You're making me nervous, Bucket."

Friday dragged on for Santiago and his men. They spent the morning going over the plans and in the afternoon, cleaned their rifles....sidearms...and checked their ammo. They had an arsenal and in the bed of each van enough explosives to set the main street of Cordes Junction on fire.

The day of the attack couldn't come soon enough for Santiago. He was ready to unleash his new gang on the town of Cordes Junction. Jackson was the worst of the bunch all right, no doubt about it, but the others weren't too far behind.

Jimmy McBride was Tennessee-born, bald, and tattoos covered most of his body. When he spoke, he had a southern drawl and Santiago was constantly having him repeat his sentences. Lucky for Santiago, McBride didn't say a lot. Instead, he sat in a chair and cracked his knuckles, smiling constantly, as if he was the only one in the world who could perform such a feat.

Chester Owens and Kip Wells were cousins and Santiago couldn't tell whether they liked each other or not. The two men grew up in Portland, Oregon and spent the better part of their lives in and out of the slammer. They certainly didn't look alike. Owens was tall and lanky, while Wells was a short and stocky. They both had the same eyes though, dark blue, but creepy. Santiago figured those two could just as easily slit your throat. Giving them a couple of sawed-off shotguns, seemed a bit of an overkill.

Santiago took a liking to Judd and Billy Bob. Judd was a young man who was born on the wrong side of the tracks, jumped a train one day and never looked back. The boy had potential. Judd had been told what to do for so long, beaten to a pulp by so many, and thrown to the wolves so many times, and now it was time for payback and he didn't care who was in front of him...they'd better move. As for Billy Bob, he was just a big old country boy. Put a baseball bat in his hands and he'd turn it into sawdust.

A group of misfits, all of them with nothing to lose...but their lives.

Johnny Sylvester sat crumpled up in a chair in the corner of his office. He had been beaten. The left side of his face was covered in blood. He couldn't take much more, but he was still thinking clearly. What they were asking him to do was possible, but dangerous. He figured if he'd agree with their plan, there'd be a chance...a slight chance he might come out of this alive.

He was an old man...too old to go up against these goons. They were both dressed in a suit and tie and they both went to great lengths to keep Johnny's blood off their clothing. The two men returned to the room and propped the crop duster up in his chair.

"Okay, I'll do it."

The man with the brass knuckles on his right hand, turned to his partner and said, "Now we're getting somewhere."

Bucket had tried his best to console Julia, tried his best to make the evening as normal as possible. He'd be leaving before sun up. He'd meet up with Wanda, the Simpson brothers and Freddie Greathouse at his office, one final preparation for the weekend. He had a skeleton crew. He new that Malfonso was predictable, just like his brothers, they'd attack out in the open.

Greathouse's men were focusing on the area near Stoney's ranch and it would be up to Freddie and the Simpson brothers to guard the entrance to town and a 10-mile stretch on I-17, north and south of the Cordes Junction off ramp.

Wanda would stay put in the office and Bucket would patrol the streets of Cordes Junction. Chances were good Santiago was counting on the element of surprise — but Bucket had planned his defense. Bucket had met with the town leaders earlier in the week, the businesses along Main Street were locked up for the next forty-eight hours, most of them were closed until Monday anyway. Bucket would worry about Monday on Monday.

Sure, there was a lot of squabbling from the business owners — especially the few who normally would have an "open for business" sign in their front window, but it didn't take much talking to convince them that their lives were at stake. Bucket was ready for another all out battle.

Santiago had done his homework. He had acquired the most recent maps for central Arizona. He had found an old mining trail. The location: just five-hundred yards north of the rental — the rental he now shared with six men. The trail led east to a dry wash which curved north under an underpass and then made its way south to the New River Mountains.

Santiago and five of his men wouldn't be going that far. They would make a detour just four miles south of Cordes Junction and make a visit to a transformer substation along the way. Santiago would detonate the first of his explosives. The power outage that followed in Cordes Junction would certainly get the attention of Sheriff Bucket Smith. Before this Bucket Smith had a chance to react, Main Street would be in flames.

Santiago would attack all right — right down the center of Main Street...his final destination: the Sheriff's office.

The young Snyder would be taking a different route. A little bit of paint and the artistic talents of Snyder left both sides of his van with the words, Cottonwood Cable Company. By the time the authorities along the highway discovered the company didn't exists, the young killer, who hated the world and everybody in it, would crash through the gate at the Johnson ranch — looking for one man and one man alone, the man with an S.J. on his belt buckle.

All along Santiago's main target wasn't Johnson, but it was

Bucket Smith — the son of Herman Smith, the man who had caused the Malfonso family grief for more than a half a century.

If Santiago survived the battle and if any of his men made it out alive, they'd roll out of town and head down Clay Road, turn on Cherry Farms Road and high tail it down a seldom-used country road which led to a drag strip out in the middle of nowhere.

There, a plane would be waiting for them — they'd board and soar to freedom — leaving behind a smoldering town below.

Bucket had done all he could to prepare for what was coming next. It was four o'clock when he arrived at his office. Julia was safe. She had her orders. "Stay put. Keep the radio turned into my frequency."

The businesses had been warned. Main Street was in lockdown. Freddie had half of his men patrolling the interstate and the remaining men focusing on the Johnson ranch. The Simpson brothers had the entrance to town covered and Bucket was third on the pecking order — protecting the streets of downtown Cordes Junction.

Maybe it would all be for nothing. Maybe, just maybe, he'd get a report this morning that Santiago had been found — captured, handcuffed and taken into custody as he tried to make his escape through the easy to get to border towns — like Nogales...maybe El Paso to the east, or maybe he fled to southern California and vanished among the millions of people in Los Angeles or San Diego. There was a report last week, he'd been spotted in Kingman, another report came in he'd been seen at a gas station on the west side of Yuma — all false alarms.

Santiago was coming to town, seeking nothing more than revenge — payback for what Bucket's father and his mother had done to the Malfonso family. Bucket just wasn't sure when, but he was prepared just the same. An inconvenience for the people of Cordes Junction for sure, but the alternative — the loss of human lives, made it a no-brainer.

The clock was ticking and Bucket's intuition was telling him Santiago was close.

It wasn't too long ago when Sergeant Theodore "Bucket"

Smith sat in a foxhole in Vietnam, preparing for an attack, an attack on his platoon — an attack which would take the lives of many of his men. Bucket never fired another shot in Vietnam — never fought another battle.

Bucket returned from the war, wounded and a mess mentally, but confident in the fact he'd raised his weapon for the last time. He was sadly mistaken.

Snyder was a loner.

The less people around him the better. The last few days with his new bunkmates had drove him up a wall. Santiago, on the other hand, had been good to him. Snyder was elated when his boss offered him the side job — take out this Johnson guy and then escape by whatever means possible.

He'd have to improvise.

If he made it out alive, Snyder would head north to Flagstaff. He'd make his way downtown to the train station. Santiago had given him a different key — a key to a locker which contained his cut and his ticket to somewhere. He would be free with enough green stuff to last him a while...and he'd be alone, just the way he liked it.

Snyder had been on the road for a couple of hours. He had backtracked west to Prescott Valley, turned north on highway 69, took the cutoff onto highway 169 and curled his way back to the interstate and within a mile of the entrance to the Johnson Ranch. He pulled over, checked his two hand guns and reached for the rifle and sawed-off shotgun in the back of the van.

He was ready. He prepared himself mentally. Images of the faces of all of those so-called human beings who had done him wrong flashed in front of him. His anger turned to rage.

He floored the gas pedal.

Snyder hit the on-ramp to I-17 and five minutes later he reached the ranch gate. He didn't bother to knock as he blasted through the entrance, heading directly for the Johnson compound.

A bullet shattered the back window of the van. Snyder glanced back and saw a Palomino, the rider atop the saddle with a rifle in his hand, preparing for another shot.

Snyder made a quick adjustment. He turned the steering wheel to the right, the next shot blasted through the front windshield. Snyder regained control of the van and sped away, now within a half a mile of the ranch.

Foreman Dusty Rhodes reached for his radio, "They're attacking, Stoney...they're attacking. It's just one van. Can't see how many are inside, but they've broken through the gate, they're just minutes from you."

Snyder looked back through his shattered back window. He saw the lights of three cars bearing down on him. "My, God. They've been waiting for me."

With blood running down the side of his face and the tip of a six-inch piece of glass lodged in his neck, he new he had been had. He screamed loudly, as he realized he was no more than a decoy for Santiago. His fiery entrance to the Johnson ranch was anything but a surprise.

Up a head he could see the figure of a tall man with a rifle in his hand. There were two men —

one on each side of him armed with shotguns. Snyder pulled the piece of glass from his neck, grabbed the shotgun and locked it into the steering wheel. With both hands free, he grabbed both pistols and fired through the space in the windshield.

Stoney and his cowhands returned fire. The last thing Snyder saw was Stoney's belt buckle.

Bullets riddled the front of the van. The vehicle rolled to the right, turned over on its side and crashed into a wagon loaded with bales of hay. The hay caught fire and Snyder's van exploded.

Three late-model sedans pulled into the compound. Three men jumped out of the vehicles and ran toward Johnson. "That was easy enough," surmised one of the FBI men. They all looked to the south and saw the smoke coming from the power plant in Cordes Junction.

"We're not the target," Stoney said with real concern on his face. Somebody radio in to Bucket...he's about to have company."

The route Santiago and his men took to the transformer substation was a rough one — potholes everywhere — cactus, rocks, everything you'd find on the desert floor; the wash was sandy with plenty of soft spots to slow them down, the embankment out of the wash was no picnic either, but somehow, someway they reached the power plant and planted the first device.

Santiago set the alarm and by the time the two vans were within a mile of the southern end of Cordes Junction, the homemade bomb had exploded, sending trails of fire and black smoke into the air.

Bucket, Wanda and Freddie Greenhouse stood on the courthouse steps. Freddie was in contact with his man who had been in charge of the surveillance out at the Johnson ranch. "The ranch was hit. One bad guy down...he was alone...everyone in one piece here, but it looks like Cordes Junction is the main target. We're heading your way, but we're pretty far out."

Freddie lowered his phone. "Santiago is here!"

Bucket radioed the Simpson boys. "Matt and Mark, I need your cruisers here, pronto!"

"We're on our way!"

"Wanda get your vehicle. I'll grab mine. We'll set up a wall of vehicles at the corner of First Avenue and Main. The plant access road turns into First Avenue. They have to come right at us."

"I'm with you, buddy," Freddie said.

"Wanda, help us get all the the remaining rifles and ammo out of the office and then I want you to get your butt off the street. Do you hear me, Wanda?"

"Yes, Bucket. I hear you."

Bucket glanced at his watch. It was seven o'clock and the sun was making its first appearance of the day, rising...slowly over the buildings, just east of town. The smoke from the power plant — curling its way into town. The traffic lights were out. Cordes Junction was without power.

The vehicles were in place. What guns and ammo they had left were handed out. The

Simpson brothers, Freddie Greathouse and Wanda prepared for battle.

"Wanda, I thought I told you..."

"There's no time," Wanda shouted as she pointed up First Avenue.

The two vans roared into town. Four armed men jumped out the back of the vans as the two drivers headed directly for Bucket's wall of vehicles. Bucket, Freddie and the Simpson brothers opened fire.

The two drivers, Wells and Owens, were hit instantly and lost control of their vans.

The Wells van rolled four times and slid through the front entrance of the Johnson hardware store...exploding, and setting off two more explosions — causing the two businesses to the west of the hardware store, Alice's Cafe and the Cordes Auto Parts, to go up in flames.

The Owen's van plowed into the road block and was sent airborne, sliding on its side down Main Street. Owens, still alive, tried his best to get out of the vehicle. He screamed as the flames overtook the cab and the van exploded.

Sorenson and McBride found safe haven on the east wall of the Valley National Bank, while Jackson made a run for it and hid in the alley next to the Randall Drug Store.

Freddie's men had arrived and they scattered in all directions in hopes of surrounding the attackers. Bucket caught a glimpse of Sorenson as he made a move to cross over to Main Street and fired one shot, hitting the big man just above his right knee,

McBride followed and Freddie put two shots in the chest of the second man. The two men yelled and charged toward what was left of the barricade as Bucket and Freddie unleashed another ray of bullets their way.

The two men fell to their knees, looked toward the morning sun and collapsed in the center of Main Street.

Shots rang out behind the drugstore and Razor Head Jackson found himself in a gun battle with two FBI agents — he wounded one, but his rifle jammed and he was hit by another ray of bullets. He fell against a wall, his head dropped and a broken neckless with a key attached fell to the ground — a key, which a few hours ago had been his key to freedom.

Bucket turned around. He looked up Main Street and up First Avenue. He surveyed the damage. He turned around and yelled, "Where's Malfonso?"

"I'm right here, Sheriff Bucket Smith. I'm right here."

Malfonso had control of Wanda. His left forearm squeezing against her neck.

"Now, I want you to slowly drop your gun to the ground and I want you to make sure your men and who ever these dudes in their black suits and ties are, to drop their weapons, too."

"Move them all out of here. Then I want you to get your cruiser and the three of us are going for a ride. Anybody follows us and this little deputy of yours, gets it first. Do you understand?"

Bucket slowly dropped his gun and his rifle to the ground and slid both of them toward Santiago.

"I, understand."

Bucket reached his cruiser, turned on the engine and backed the vehicle slowly toward Santiago and Wanda.

"Matt and Mark get everybody back. Give us some room and no one is to follow us."

The cruiser sped away. Bucket looked through the rearview mirror. Santiago sat in the backseat with the barrel of a sawed-off shotgun pointed right at Wanda's head.

Bucket turned the cruiser around and headed down Clay Road.

"Oh, and Mr. Smith, make a turn at Cherry Farms Road."

The Simpson brothers and Freddie Greathouse had survived the battle. Luckily, the only injury was to one FBI agent who took a bullet to his right shoulder on a shotgun blast from Razor Head Jackson.

They all stood, with their weapons at their side, and watched Bucket's cruiser head down Clay Road. The Simpson

Brothers knew full well there was no way out for Malfonso — the only way out of Cordes Junction was to the west and he would need to double back and take one of the side streets and hook up with I-17, unless he had another plan in place.

The men heard the sound of a vehicle entering Main Street from the west. Suddenly a Willys Jeep rolled to a stop and Stoney Johnson exited the vehicle and ran over to the edge of the barricade.

"What's going on?" yelled Stoney.

"Malfonso escaped and he's taken Bucket and Wanda hostage," answered Freddie. "They sped off in Buckct's cruiser. Bucket said to stay back or Malfonso would kill them both."

"My, God! There's nothing out there, but a 10-mile stretch down Cherry Farms Road. Where are they going? Where's the rest of Malfonso's men?

"We got 'em all Stoney...they're all dead." Matt said.

"You can add one more to the list. There's a dead man back at the ranch."

"Mark said, "We can't just stand here. We gotta do something!"

Greathouse made a decision. "Let's get two of my men up here. Let's take two of our cars and we'll follow them and stay out of sight. Looks like the fire department has things under control here."

Stoney turned and for the first time realized his hardware store was gone and the buildings along the entire block were smoldering. "We can always rebuild, but it's the lives of Bucket and Wanda I'm concerned about…and Julia! My God, she's out at the house at the end of Cherry Farms Road."

Bucket tried his best to keep his cruiser in a straight line. He looked through the rear view mirror and watched Malfonso continue to push the barrel of the shotgun deeper into Wanda's neck. She continued to call out, "Please don't hurt me."

"Hurt you. I need to keep you alive, you're my ticket out of here, along with the other filly at the end of this road."

Bucket's worst fear. Malfonso knew everything. He turned on to Cherry Farms road. He floored the gas pedal.

"There's no way I'm handing over Julia to you!"

"We'll see about that," yelled Malfonso as he eased up his hold on Wanda and with his right hand he grabbed a hold of Bucket's shirt collar. Wanda, realizing this was her chance, raised her right leg and with with all the force she could muster — kicked the shotgun loose.

"Damn you!" Malfonso bellowed, as he reached down to regain his weapon. Bucket quickly turned the wheel sharply to the right. The cruiser rolled over once, twice — the back window shattered and Wanda was ejecting as the vehicle began to spin, upside down, with Bucket and Malfonso battling for the shotgun.

Bucket broke free and pounded his right fist into the side of Malfonso's head...once...twice...three times. Bucket grabbed the shotgun and threw it out the side window. The engine caught fire and Bucket had just seconds to pull his body through the rear window, broken glass tearing into his skin as he eased his way out of the vehicle.

The heat was unbearable as Bucket got to his feet, ran ten yards and vaulted into the air. The cruiser exploded for the second time and flames were sent in all directions.

The last of the Malfonso brothers trapped — unable to escape the burning wreckage.

"Bucket are you alright?"

"I'm, okay. I'm okay, are you alright, Wanda?"

"I'm alive, Bucket...I'm alive. How did we survive?"

"I don't know, Wanda. It just wasn't our time."

Bucket looked past the burning squad car, desperately trying to get his bearings. He was just one-hundred yards from the entrance to his farm house. He could see a figure running toward him. His eyes blurry, he began to focus as Julia bolted into his arms.

"Bucket, you're alive!"

Two vehicles rolled to a stop. Stoney Johnson and Freddie Greathouse and four FBI agents emerged from the vehicles. Freddie reached the wreckage first, turned to Bucket and said, "Old buddy, the stuff you get yourself into!"

Bucket looked to the south. "Quiet. Listen!"

A plane, the engines sputtering, suddenly appeared and headed directly for the giant oak tree in the front of the Cherry

Farms homestead. The left wing of the aircraft clipped the top of the tree, a trail of smoke followed as the Beechcraft Queen Air crashed into the open field.

"Jesus!" What's next? Bucket said, as he motioned to the men, "Let's roll!"

Bucket, Freddie and his men reached the wreckage site in minutes. The plane was still smoldering, oil and gas everywhere. They quickly pulled three bodies from the aircraft and dragged them away from the plane.

"They're gone. Looks like a pilot and two well-dressed men."

"This was supposed to be Malfonso's way out of here. They we're heading for the drag strip, Bucket surmised.

The plane exploded.

"They didn't make it. Case closed," said Freddie Greathouse.

## Chapter 9

A week later…

Bucket said goodbye to Julia.

He kissed her and promised to be home early for dinner. He drove west on Cherry Farms Road. He passed the spot where Santiago Malfonso had met his maker — no remnants of what happen there existed, no evidence on the ground, leaving a clue as to what had occurred there.

Bucket smiled. Julia was safe and she had her day planned. She would plant another row of rose bushes before the sun found its way over the top of the Green River Mountains. She would ride into town and have her hair done and then ride out to the Cordes Junction Cemetery and place a single rose in front of the gravestone of her beloved Maggie. She'd then kneel down and place another rose near the gravesite of Maggie's partner in crime, sweet Mildred.

Wanda, with her right arm and left leg in a cast, stood by the bus stop with her three children. It was the first day of school and the yellow school bus would be arriving soon. She looked down at her children. They had their lunch buckets and their light jackets. It was a cool, crisp morning...and everything was back to normal.

The Simpson brothers were out on patrol. Tilly was up a tree again and a family of four had blown an engine in their van, two miles west of the Prescott turnoff.

With his left arm in a sling and his midsection heavily wrapped, Bucket was still able to maneuver his new but slightly used cruiser — on loan from the Prescott Valley Police Department — through the downtown area of Cordes. Bucket drove by what was to be Stoney Johnson's brand new hardware store — the foundation was in, and according to the construction boss, "Stoney would be back in business by late October."

Bucket slowed down his cruiser and peeked out the window. Sure enough, Alice had her new sign up, advertising the best pies in the county.

Alice would be serving her pies in less than two weeks and the rest of the office buildings on the north side of Main Street received very little damage, and would be open for business by the end of the week.

Workers from the Arizona Public Service had worked day and night since the explosion at the substation and electricity was restored less than twenty-four hours after Malfonso and his men had done their dirty work.

Bucket had reached his office. He parked in his assigned spot and walked the dozen steps to his office. There was a note on his desk from Freddie Greathouse. "Please stay out of trouble. Keep in touch. I'll see you at the 10-year reunion."

Bucket chuckled and poured himself a cup of coffee He looked out the window. A semi truck had just arrived with a load of wood. Bucket figured Stoney's insurance company would be writing out plenty of checks. Bucket looked next door. Alice had just pulled up, got out of her old, but well-kept Plymouth and began to issue orders to a painter on just how she wanted the lettering to flow in the front window of her establishment.

As for Stoney Johnson. He was going to take it easy. He surprised Alexandra and the entire Johnson family by handing them round-trip tickets to Italy — including a two-week stay with his wife's family in Bali. Mary Hamilton would be around to monitor the progress on the rebuilding of the hardware store and Stoney handed over the reigns at the ranch to his foreman, Dusty Rhodes.

Bucket would stay put and keep his boots on the ground and enjoy some quiet, peaceful days in Cordes Junction. Was there really such a thing? he muttered.

Bucket eyed the front pages of the five newspapers on his desk.

The headline of the Arizona Republic read: *Crop Duster Dies in Plane Crash.*

Bucket discovered through police reports that two of Santiago's hired guns had forced a man named Johnny Sylvester, an aging crop duster, to fly his plane from Goodyear to the isolated drag strip — the getaway plane for Malfonso and his men.

According to information retrieved from the flight recorder and from autopsy records, Sylvester died of a heart attack and the two men on board the aircraft died of trauma, more than likely they died at impact. The last human voice echoed over the airways was likely one of the gunmen, "We're going down!"

The headline in the Phoenix Gazette read: *Son of Crime Boss dies in Car Crash.*

Bucket, tossed the Gazette on his desk. It was painful to watch a man die. Malfonso was a killer, but he was a human being and he died a horrible death. Bucket had read the Greathouse file on Santiago — it wasn't pretty. From childhood to manhood — the man was caught in a trap — a trap which eventually led to his death.

The Prescott Courier headline read, *Terror in Cordes Junction*, while the Camp Verde Times reported, *Sheriff Saves Arizona Town,* and up in Las Vegas the daily paper read, *Last of the Malfonso brothers dies in Arizona Gun Battle.*

Bucket Smith shook his head and focused on the pile of paperwork on his desk. He looked at the clock. He could almost smell the aroma of Julia's pork chops.

*****